*Witchblade* created by:
Marc Silvestri, David Wohl,
Brian Haberlin and Michael Turner

published by
Top Cow Productions, Inc.
Los Angeles

# WITCHBLADE®

## ORIGINS
### VOLUME 1

# WITCHBLADE®

For Top Cow Productions, Inc.:
**Marc Silvestri** - Chief Executive Officer
**Matt Hawkins** - President and Chief Operating Officer
**Filip Sablik** - Publisher
**Phil Smith** - Managing Editor
**Bryan Rountree** - Assistant to the Publisher
**Christine Dinh** - Marketing Assistant
**Mark Haynes** - Webmaster
**Ryan Anderson, Ernest Gomez, Anthony McAfee** - Interns

for *image* comics
publisher:
Eric Stephenson

letters for all issues in this edition by:
**Dennis Heisler**

Want more info? check out:
***www.topcow.com*** and ***www.thetopcowstore.com***
for news and exclusive Top Cow merchandise!

For this edition
Cover art by:
Michael Turner, D-Tron and JD Smith

For this edition
Book Design and Layout by:
Phil Smith

**Witchblade: Origins volume 1 Trade Paperback**
**May 2010. SECOND PRINTING. ISBN: 978-1-58240-901-6**
Published by Image Comics Inc. Office of Publication: 1942 University Ave., Suite 305 Berkeley, CA 94704. $14.99 U.S.D.. Originally published in single magazine form as WITCHBLADE 1-8. 

# TABLE OF CONTENTS

# ISSUE #1

co-plot: **David Wohl** and **Brian Haberlin**
script: **David Wohl** with **Christina Z.**
pencils and co-plot: **Michael Turner**
inks: **D-Tron**
colors: **JD Smith** and **Nathan Cabrera**

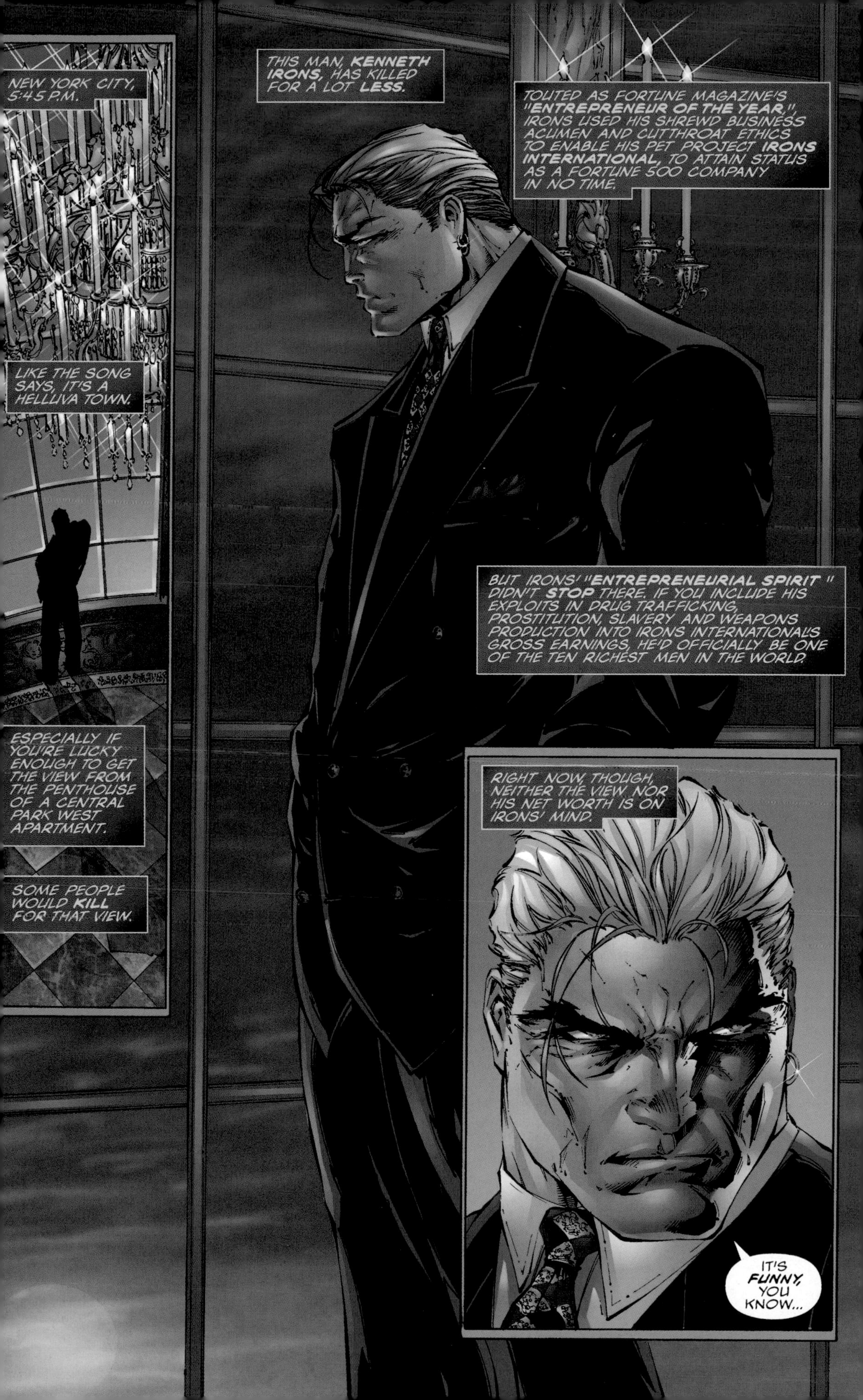
NEW YORK CITY, 5:45 P.M.
LIKE THE SONG SAYS, IT'S A HELLUVA TOWN.
ESPECIALLY IF YOU'RE LUCKY ENOUGH TO GET THE VIEW FROM THE PENTHOUSE OF A CENTRAL PARK WEST APARTMENT.
SOME PEOPLE WOULD KILL FOR THAT VIEW.
THIS MAN, KENNETH IRONS, HAS KILLED FOR A LOT LESS.
TOUTED AS FORTUNE MAGAZINE'S "ENTREPRENEUR OF THE YEAR", IRONS USED HIS SHREWD BUSINESS ACUMEN AND CUTTHROAT ETHICS TO ENABLE HIS PET PROJECT IRONS INTERNATIONAL, TO ATTAIN STATUS AS A FORTUNE 500 COMPANY IN NO TIME.
BUT IRONS' "ENTREPRENEURIAL SPIRIT" DIDN'T STOP THERE. IF YOU INCLUDE HIS EXPLOITS IN DRUG TRAFFICKING, PROSTITUTION, SLAVERY AND WEAPONS PRODUCTION INTO IRONS INTERNATIONAL'S GROSS EARNINGS, HE'D OFFICIALLY BE ONE OF THE TEN RICHEST MEN IN THE WORLD.
RIGHT NOW, THOUGH, NEITHER THE VIEW NOR HIS NET WORTH IS ON IRONS' MIND.
IT'S FUNNY, YOU KNOW...

OCCUPYING HIS THOUGHTS TONIGHT IS THE SAME ITEM THAT HE'S COVETED FOR THE GREATER PART OF HIS ADULT LIFE.
...I PROBABLY KNOW MORE ABOUT YOU THAN ANYONE ALIVE.
IT'S WHAT, UNBEKNOWNST TO HIS STOCKHOLDERS, HE'S DEVOTED HIMSELF TO.
IT'S WHAT, UNBEKNOWNST TO THE COLUMNISTS WHO ELECTED HIM ONE OF NEW YORK'S MOST ELIGIBLE BACHELORS, HE'S DEVOTED HIS LOVE TO.
I KNOW NEARLY EVERY PLACE YOU'VE EVER BEEN... WHO'S HELD YOU... WHO'S BEEN HURT BY YOU...
UNFORTUNATELY, THIS DEVOTION IS UNREQUITED.
BUT SINCE I CAN NEVER HAVE YOU, THESE TOURNAMENTS MUST CONTINUE-- UNTIL I FIND THE ONE WHO CAN.
THE OBJECT OF HIS DESIRE DOESN'T CARE ABOUT HIM OR HIS LOVE.

I FEEL TONIGHT IT MAY FINALLY HAPPEN. YOUR WIELDER WILL REVEAL HIMSELF.
BUT, LIKE MOST BAD RELATIONSHIPS, THE TORTURED PARTNER KEEPS COMING BACK.
EVEN THOUGH HE KNOWS HE CAN NEVER HAVE IT, IRONS HAS SEEN A HINT OF ITS POWER--AND THAT'S ENOUGH TO ENSURE A LIFETIME OF ARDOR--
--AND PAIN.
THEN I WILL OWN YOU BOTH.
AS A MATTER OF FACT, IT ABHORS HIM. THE ONE TIME HE TRIED TO TOUCH IT, IT SHOWED HIM HOW MUCH.

CHELSEA. 5:45 P.M.
IT WAS **STARSKY AND HUTCH** THAT DID IT. BY THE END OF THE SHOW, IN THAT RED TORINO, THEY ALWAYS GOT THE BAD GUY.
EVEN WHEN I WAS A LITTLE GIRL, **I KNEW** I WAS GONNA BE A COP.
IN THIRD GRADE, MY BEST FRIEND LEE AND I USED TO PRETEND WE WERE SARA STARSKY AND LEE HUTCH.
LEE'S MARRIED NOW AND LIVING IN, WHERE IS IT, **TEANECK**--I THINK.
dogs
mr. blonde
I RECALL READING A FEW YEARS BACK THAT STARSKY'S WIFE DIED OF A.I.D.S. **DAMN.**
AND **ME?** OH, I GET TO WEAR DRESSES THAT MY MOM WOULD **SLAP** ME FOR --IF SHE WERE STILL HERE.

HEY! WHO'S THE--
I WORK IN A SYSTEM THAT FAVORS THE GUILTY--WHETHER THEY'RE DOUBLE-MURDERERS IN L.A. OR CONNIVING DRUG DEALERS HERE ON MY BEAT--AS LONG AS THEY HAVE THE CASH... THEY'LL WALK.
UNFORTUNATELY FOR THE LATTER, MONEY DOESN'T ALWAYS TALK LOUD ENOUGH.
NATE
YOU JUST CAN'T BE GOING AROUND MURDERING PEOPLE-- ESPECIALLY THE WOMAN I USED TO PLAY HAND-BALL WITH IN SCHOOL.
HER LIFE WAS WORTH MORE THAN WHAT THIS CREEP DID TO HER.
GRAMERCY PARK. 6:13 P.M.
1169
THE JURY MAY HAVE LET HIM GO--BUT THAT DOESN'T MEAN I HAVE TO.
STARSKY NEVER HAD TO DO THIS TO MAKE A BUST.

THEN AGAIN, HE COULDN'T
GUESS I'M IN THE RIGHT PLACE.
SMELLS LIKE A CHEESY BAR BATHROOM.
DREXLER HERE TELLS ME YER LOOKIN' TO DROP SOME HORSE.
WELL, I'VE HAD SOME TROUBLE WITH RATS LATELY.
YES, WELL--MY CLIENT HAS SOME PRESSING BUSINESS AND NEEDS CAPITAL. I'M PREPARED TO OFFER FIRE SALE PRICES ON 125 KILOS OF QUALITY MERCHANDISE.
REALLY--MUST BE MY LUCKY DAY, HUH, BLITZ?
YRRHMM...
FORGIVE ME IF I'M A LITTLE WARY. A GUY DOESN'T GET TO WHERE I AM TRUSTING EVERY SHORT SKIRT THAT WALKS THROUGH THE DOOR...
OH, PUH-LEASE.
SO... DO WE CLOSE?

URINE, SWEAT AND BEER. NOTHING BUT THE BEST FOR GALLO.
YOU'RE MS. FORTRAN?
MATTER A' FACT, I THINK THERE'S ONE HERE RIGHT NOW! IF WE'RE GONNA "CLOSE," THEN YOU GOTTA TAKE CARE OF THIS LITTLE PROBLEM.
KCHANK!
I KNOW YOU GOT A PIECE. USE IT--
--ON HIM!
THIS SHOULD BE INTERESTING.
WHATTA YA MEAN ON HIM--ME-- HEY! WAIT UP!
HMMM... SUCH A HANDSOME FACE...
...TOO BAD.

OODGHPD...
KRAAKK!
NOT TOO MANY CHICKS CAN PULL THE TRIGGER, BUT NICE MOVE ANYWAY. YOU'RE ALL--WAIT--I, UH, KNOW YOU...
KCHUKT
COOL.
THESE DAYS, COPS ARE SWITCHING TO .45 AUTOMATICS. I COULD NEVER DO THAT.

FEW THINGS MATCH THE FEELING OF FIRING A .357 SNUB-NOSED SWING-OUT **REVOLVER.**
THE PISTOL IS LIKE PART OF MY **HAND.** WITH IT, I'M A **SUPER-HERO...**
BLAM!
...BLASTING THE BAD GUYS WITH MY **FIREBALLS OF JUSTICE.**
PCHUK!
BRINGING MEN TO THEIR KNEES.

STARSKY'D BE PROUD!
RECOGNIZE ME NOW, YOU PIECE OF $#!&?
P--PEZZINI.
OH--YOU FLATTER ME. OF COURSE. I WAS ON YOUR MURDER CASE.
YOU KILLED A FRIEND OF MINE DURING YOUR LAST TURF WAR. MARIA BUZANIS--
--WHO STUPIDLY THOUGHT SHE COULD TAKE AN AFTERNOON STROLL WITH HER DAUGHTER.
YOU SHOWED HER--DIDN'T YOU? AND YOU SHOWED HER KID, WHO STOOD AND WATCHE HER MOM BLEED TO DEATH.
YOU DON'T LOOK SO GOOD, GALLO.
AND THAT COMPLEXION? YES, WELL...
I'D LAY OFF THE GREASY FOOD IF I WERE YOU.
YOUR LAWYERS AREN'T GONNA GET YOU OFF THIS TIME, GALLO. I'M GONNA ENJOY WATCHING YOU BLEED...
OH GOD NO...DON KI--
POLICE! HANDS IN THE--
KRASHHKK
HOLD YOUR FIRE. READ THIS GUY HIS RIGHTS. AND DON'T LEAVE ANYTHING OUT THIS TIME.
I DIDN'T KNOW PEZ WAS INVITED TO THIS LITTLE PARTY, JAKE.
NEITHER DID I-- BUT IT LOOKS LIKE SHE'S DRESSED FOR IT!

LONG ISLAND CITY. 6:41 P.M.
TWENTY-FIVE YEARS AGO, THE RIALTO THEATER WAS A SHINING SPIRE IN THIS BUSTLING NEIGHBORHOOD.
BUT A DECADE OF EVER-GROWING DRUG PEDDLING AND PROSTITUTION ON THESE STREETS LED TO THE CLOSING OF THIS FORMER LANDMARK.
TWENTY-FIVE YEARS AGO, TONY CUGLIANI WAS ONE OF THE MOST POWERFUL CRIME BOSSES IN QUEENS. THREE DIFFERENT NEIGHBORHOODS BOTH CELEBRATED AND LIVED IN FEAR OF HIS EVERY WORD.
BUT A DECADE OF ARRIVING IMMIGRANTS, WITH THEIR OWN ORGANIZED CRIME FAMILIES, RIDDLED CUGLIANI'S POWER BASE. NOW THE RASPY-VOICED ITALIAN-AMERICAN HOLDS ONLY A FEW BLOCKS AT BAY...
AH, MR., UH, CUGLIANI-- WELCOME TO THE TOURNAMENT.
YOUR ENTRY FEE, PLEASE?
DAT'S BEIN' HELD BY DIS LOVELY LADY RIGHT--HEY, WATCH YER HANDS!
THANK YOU, MR. CUGLIANI. YOU CAN GO.
DIS IS GONNA BE MY LUCKY NIGHT, SOFIE.
THANKS TO KENNETH IRONS' TOURNAMENT, BOTH THE MAN AND THE THEATER ARE GETTING THE CHANCE TO RELIVE THEIR FORMER GLORIES.
MY LUCKY NIGHT...

HEADQUARTERS. 6:42 P.M.
I'LL ASK YOU AGAIN. JUST WHAT IN THE HELL WERE YOU DOING IN THERE, PEZZINI?
ARE YOU LISTENING TO ME?
THE GUY WITH THE CIGARETTE, ROLLED-UP SLEEVES AND ULTRA-HIGH BLOOD PRESSURE IS MY BOSS, LIEUTENANT JOE SIRY.
I CAN'T LOOK UP AT HIM RIGHT NOW BECAUSE THE VEIN THAT POPS OUT ON HIS FOREHEAD WHILE HE'S ANGRY ALWAYS MAKES ME LAUGH.
AND HE PROBABLY WOULDN'T APPRECIATE THAT--BEING THE CHIEF, AND ALL.
YES, SIR.
YOU ENDANGERED PEOPLE'S LIVES, INTRUDED ON NARCOTICS OFFICERS' TERRITORY, DRESSED LIKE A SLUT--
HEY! YOU THINK I LIKE WEARING THIS?
I THOUGHT SHE LOOKED HOT...
I...UHM... MAYBE...HEY, JOHN, I'LL HELP YOU WITH THOSE FINGERPRINTS!
GET IN MY OFFICE, PEZZINI!
NOW!
AFTER THAT, YOU CAN FILE YOUR REPORT WITH ME. I'M SURE IT'LL BE INTERESTING.
I CAN HARDLY WAIT...
THAT'S SELZER, OUR RESIDENT INTERNAL AFFAIRS SLIMEBALL. THAT EXPRESSION ON HIS FACE IS THE CLOSEST HE'LL EVER GET TO A SMILE.

AND...
SO LET ME TRY TO FIGURE THIS-- YOU TALK YOUR PARTNER INTO HELPING YOU WITH THIS SCHEME, THEN YOU PISTOL-WHIP HIM? JUST WHAT ARE YOU--
--WELL, YEAH, BUT IT SOUNDS WORSE THAN IT IS.
LOOK, SARA, I KNOW YOU'RE UPSET THAT GALLO GOT OFF BEFORE, BUT YOU GOTTA STOP THIS VENDETTA CRAP! YOU MAY HAVE NAILED HIM THIS TIME...
JOE'S THE CLOSEST THING I HAVE TO FAMILY THESE DAYS. HE CARES FOR ME, AND I GIVE HIM GRIEF.
...BUT YOU'RE GETTING RECKLESS, AND THAT SCARES ME.
THE PERFECT FATHER/DAUGHTER RELATIONSHIP.
ANYTHING ELSE, CHIEF?
JUST KEEP YOUR HEAD STRAIGHT OUT THERE. WELL, LOOKS LIKE YOUR PARTNER'S OUT OF THE INFIRMARY. YEE, CHIN UP! SOME PEOPLE PAY FOR WHAT SHE DID TO YOU...
HEY, YEE, HOW'S THE OLD NOGGIN?
UH, FINE. DREXLER'S READY FOR US IN INTERROGATION ROOM TWO.
I THINK YEE'S MAD AT ME. WONDER IF THANKING HIM FOR BEING A TEAM PLAYER WOULD HELP.
PROBABLY NOT.

HEAT'S PUMPED UP IN THE INTERROGATION ROOM TO MAKE IT ALMOST LIKE A SAUNA. WE COPS ARE USED TO IT.
SORRY IT'S SO HOT IN HERE, DREX. YA KNOW, YOU REALLY HELPED US NAIL GALLO, DIDN'T YOU?
T'WEREN'T NOTHIN', PEZ. GUY WAS CREEPIN' ME OUT, ANYWAY...
WHY'S THAT?
OH, SO... UH...HEY, WELL, YOU KNOW, I THINK HE WAS DOIN' TOO MUCH SAMPLIN'!
REALLY? THAT'S IT?
INTERROGATION RULE NUMBER NINE--EVERYBODY KNOWS MORE THAN THEY'RE TELLING. DREXLER'S A GOOD INFORMANT, BUT SOMETIMES HE'S RELUCTANT TO SPILL IT ALL. SOMETIMES, HE NEEDS SOME...PRODDING.
WELL, WHY DID HE WANT TO SEE ME? HE'S SMALL CHANGE. THE STUFF I WAS SELLING WAS WAY OUTTA HIS LEAGUE.
HMM...
LOOKED TO ME LIKE HE NEEDED BIG BUCKS FAST-- WANTED TO MAKE A KILLING. WHY?
COULDN'T TELL YA.
REALLY? YOU CAN'T? OH...
...I THINK YOU CAN!
NOW, YOU WANNA TELL ME WHAT GALLO WAS GONNA DO WITH THAT MONEY, DREX? YEE--LOCK THE DOOR...
UNGH... I...STTOPPP... DUNNO... HHELLLPP...
DAMMIT, PEZ, HE SAYS HE DOESN'T KNOW!
GNNRLGH...OKAY... HE SAID SOMETHIN' 'BOUT SOME ENTRY FEE... CKLNGD. BIG EVENT DOWN AT THE OLD RITZ, RHODIE...NO--TH-- THE RIALTO!
I GUESS THIS MEANS I CAN'T HURT YOU, DREX. YOU WIN.
UM, DETECTIVES PEZZINI, YEE? YOU GUYS HAVE A NEW CASE.
IN PRAISE OF PRODDING...

7:15P.M. RIALTO THEATER.
MR. IRONS, I'VE CONFIRMED YOUR MEETING WITH PRESIDENT HUSSEIN AT 7P.M., IRAQI TIME, TOMORROW EVENING. WE FLY OUT AFTER THE TOURNAMENT.
IT SEEMS HE WANTS TO SET UP A "DINNER" BETWEEN YOU AND HIS DAUGHTER...
OH, ANOTHER DINNER WITH SOME PRESIDENT'S DAUGHTER. WHAT DO YOU THINK OF MY CROWD, NOTTINGHAM?
THERE ARE A FEW FINE-LOOKING COMPETITORS, SIR.
THE "WINNER" WILL BE AMONG THEM --I KNOW IT.
SIR, MIGHT I UMBLY SUGGEST YOU NOT PLACE ALL OF YOUR CONFIDENCE IN ONE NIGHT'S TOURNAMENT? AS YOU KNOW, YOU'VE NEVER FOUND ANYONE WHO--
REVEAL MY PRIZE, NOTTINGHAM. I MISS LOOKING AT IT.
AND DO MAKE PREPARATIONS TO ACCOMMODATE OUR "WINNER."
HRRM...AS YOU WISH, SIR.

GREENWICH VILLAGE. 7:19 P.M.
TO ME, THE TWO HARDEST PARTS OF BEING A HOMICIDE DETECTIVE ARE NOTIFYING THE NEXT OF KIN AND EXAMINING THE CRIME SCENE.
POLICE
POLICE
POLICE LINE DO NOT CROSS
AFTER HEARING THE CAUSE OF DEATH AND WHO THE VICTIM WAS, I CAN'T HELP BUT IMAGINE WHAT THE ROOM WILL LOOK LIKE.
WAS THERE A STRUGGLE INVOLVED? WAS ROBBERY THE MOTIVE? DRUGS? DID THEY TRASH THE PLACE?
NO. THIS ISN'T WHAT I PICTURED AT ALL.
THIS PLACE LOOK LIKE IT WAS CLEA THIS MORNING. I WISH I WERE THA METICULOUS. NEV KNOW WHO MIGH BE EXAMINING YO APARTMENT...
CLEANLINESS DIDN'T KEEP THIS WOMAN ALIVE, THOU
FORENSICS SAYS THE KILLER PUT HER IN THIS POSITION AFTER THE MURDER.
THEY SAY SHE WAS BURNED FROM THE INSIDE OUT. KINDA LIKE A MICROWAVE OVEN.
HOW COULD SOMEONE BURN LIKE THAT? IT'S JUST NOT POSSIBLE.
SAME M.O. AS LAST WEEK'S FIND.
SEEMS WE HAVE NEW YORK'S NEWEST SERIAL KILLER ON THE LOOSE.

7:33 P.M.
IF I WERE YOU, I'D BE MORE CONCERNED WITH MY BEHAVIOR DURING OUR LITTLE EXCHANGE. IT WAS KINDA CUTE THE WAY YOU STUMBLED OVER YOUR WORDS...
OH COME ON! YOU WANNA TALK HEAT OF THE MOMENT? THREE GUNS WERE POINTED AT ME. ONE UNDER MY JAW. I DIDN'T KNOW WHICH ONE OF YOU WAS GONNA PLUG ME!
RELAX, MICHAEL, I WAS IN CONTROL THE WHOLE TIME.
WHAT'S THE DEAL, PEZ? I PUT MY LIFE ON THE LINE FOR YOUR PERSONAL RETRIBUTION AND YOU RETURN THE FAVOR BY TRYING TO KILL ME!
IT'S A CRUEL WORLD, YEE. I'M JUST PREPARING YOU FOR IT.
I'LL BUY THE BOOK. NEXT TIME WARN ME FIRST. AND WHILE YOU'RE AT IT, YOU CAN TELL ME WHERE WE'RE GOING BECAUSE--
--AW PEZ, COME ON. NOT THE RIALTO.
IT WAS IMPORTANT TO GALLO. I HAVE TO SEE WHY.
HEY, CHECK IT OUT! WHAT'S GOING ON HERE? WE SHOULD PROBABLY CALL FOR SOME--
--I'M JUST GONNA TAKE A QUICK LOOK. IF I'M NOT BACK IN FIVE MINUTES, CALL FOR BACK-UP.
TAKE MY JACKET. *SIGH* GLAD I HAVEN'T HAD A CHANCE TO TAKE THIS DRESS OFF YET!
KEEP A LOW PROFILE, SARA! OH, HEY--DID YOU REALLY MEAN IT WHEN YOU SAID I WAS HANDSOME?
YOU KNOW--HEAT OF THE MOMENT...BE RIGHT BACK.
YEE'S A GOOD GUY. MAYBE I WAS A BIT ROUGH ON HIM--
RIALTO

--WHEN THIS IS OVER, I'LL HAVE TO GET HIM A BEER. RIGHT NOW THOUGH, I HEAR OPPORTUNITY KNOCKING...
AND YOU ARE...
AHM--
WAIT FOR ME, HON...
AHM--AHM... SAM TABB. AND THIS LITTLE LADY IS, UH, MAH PERTY ESCORT.
THANK YOU, AND GOOD LUCK, SIR.
WELL, GLAD TO HAVE YAH --HUH?
I'LL HAVE TO SEND A THANK YOU NOTE TO VERSACE TOMORROW. THIS DRESS HAS REALLY COME IN... WAIT...WHAT THE HELL'S GOING ON IN HERE?
THIS THEATER'S BEEN CLOSED SINCE BEFORE I WAS BORN. LOOKS LIKE SOMEONE REMODELED.
AND ALL THESE PEOPLE. I RECOGNIZE SOME OF THEM --FROM MUG SHOTS AND FBI WIRES!
AND THAT ONE ONSTAGE--HE'S INTENSE! I GOTTA GET A CLOSER LOOK AT THIS.
GOOD EVENING, AND WELCOME TO THE TOURNAMENT. I'M IAN NOTTINGHAM, AND I'LL OVERSEE THIS EVENING'S EVENT.
YOU OBVIOUSLY KNOW WHY YOU'RE HERE, SO, WITHOUT FURTHER ADO...
...THE WITCHBLADE
THE RULES OF THIS CONTEST ARE QUITE SIMPLE. I'LL CALL YOUR NAME AND YOU'LL PLACE YOUR RIGHT HAND IN THE GAUNTLET. YOU'LL KNOW QUICKLY IF YOU'VE WON...OR NOT.
THIS IS A SICK TWIST ON A GAME SHOW. BUT I'LL TAKE THAT NOTTINGHAM GUY OVER BOB BARKER ANY DAY!
AND TONIGHT'S FIRST CONTESTANT IS... MR. TONY CUGLIANI.

ITH THE AUDIENCE EVEALED TO ITS SUPER-ATURAL SENSES, THE ITCHBLADE SCANS THE HEATER, TRYING, AS IT'S ONE COUNTLESS TIMES EFORE, TO LOCATE ITS IGHTFUL WIELDER--
YO! OVER HERE, IAN? TELL EVERYONE ELSE TA GIVE UP BECAUSE TONY CUGLIANI'S BRINGIN' HOME DA PRIZE!
HMPH. RIGHT.
AND, FOR THE FIRST TIME IN OVER 50 YEARS, IT AGITATES IN A MANNER IMPERCEPTIBLE TO ALL BUT ONE MAN IN THE THEATER.
TONY CUGLIANI? THAT GUY'S BEEN A NEW YORK FIXTURE FROM AS FAR BACK AS I CAN REMEMBER. I THOUGHT HE WAS DEAD!
YESSSS! I KNEW IT! BRING ME THE ONE, WITCHBLADE!
THAT'S RIGHT. PLACE YOUR HAND--
--I KNEW IT! FITS LIKE A--
GLAAAAAAA!
OHMIGOD!
AWWW...LET'S HAVE A HAND FOR MR. CUGLIANI...
NEXT...WE HAVE--HMM... IT APPEARS WE HAVE A VISITOR.
NO.

IT APPEARS WE HAVE A MEMBER OF NEW YORK'S FINEST IN OUR MIDST.
NO--WHY DIDN'T YOU WAIT?!?
MY FRIEND, YOU ARE TRESPASSING HERE.
A LITTLE SIDE-SHOW AT NO EXTRA CHARGE, LADIES AND GENTLEMEN. OH I SEE YOU ALL FEEL THE SAME WAY I DO--
JUST...KILL ME AND GET IT OVER WITH...
HOW TOUCHING. IF YOU INSIST. OPEN FIRE, GENTLEMEN.
WHAT?!?
KCHAK!
NOOOO!!
KCHAK!
KERRAKA!
OOOLPH...
UNGH...
MORTALLY WOUNDED, PEZ INSTINCTIVELY REACHES OUT, HOPING A GUN, A KNIFE, ANYTHING...
BUT WHAT SHE FINDS IS INFINITELY MORE MIRACULOUS THAN ANYTHING SHE COULD HAVE EVER EXPECTED.

NO! IT CAN'T **END** LIKE THIS!
THERE'S TOO MUCH LEFT TO **FIGHT** FOR!
I HAVEN'T BEEN A **HERO** YET!
**YES!** PREPARE TO TAKE HER DOWN, MEN...
I NEED MORE **TIME!**
I...
...NEED...
...TO...
...**FIGHT!**
I'M ALIVE--
--AND **KICKING!**

I AM THE LIGHT.
I AM AN ANGEL OF DEATH.
I AM POWER.

THIS IS FREEDOM.
YOU ARE **EVERYTHING** I THOUGHT YOU'D BE, WITCHBLADE. AND I'LL **POSSESS** YOU AS I'M MEANT TO! WELCOME BACK...
I AM--
--INSANE!

NO. GOTTA BE OKAY.
GOTTA--
PEZ?
YEE-- MICHAEL-- WHY DID YOU--
I...CHK ...WANTED TO SEE IF YOU WERE ALL RIGHT.
DO YOU... CHKL...STILL THINK I'M H-HANDSOME?
SNFF YES, YES.
I DO...
WHEN I WAS A LITTLE GIRL I WISHED I HAD THE POWER TO MOW DOWN ALL THE PEOPLE I THOUGHT WERE BAD SO NONE OF THEM COULD HURT ME.
NOW, SOMEHOW, I HAVE THAT POWER.
AND I'M SCARED.
THE BEGINNING.

# ISSUE #2

co-plot: **David Wohl** and **Brian Haberlin**
script: **David Wohl** with **Christina Z.**
pencils and co-plot: **Michael Turner**
inks: **D-Tron**
colors: **JD Smith** and **Nathan Cabrera**

NEW YORK CITY. 10:30P.M.
WHEN THE NEW YORK TIMES GOT A TIP ON WHAT WENT DOWN AT THE HONEY POT NIGHT CLUB, THEY IMMEDIATELY SENT A REPORTER AND PHOTOGRAPHER TO INVESTIGATE.
HEY, HONEY, YOU AWAKE IN THERE?
THE NEW YORK POST GOT THERE FIRST, THOUGH. AND, UPON HEARING WHAT HAPPENED, THEY PULLED THIS MORNING'S EDITION OFF THE PRESSES.
RESTROOM
IS SHE OUT YET?
YEAH-- I GOTTA GO!
TOMORROW THE POST'S READERS WERE SUPPOSED TO SEE THE HEADLINE "PRINCESS DI'S NYC TRYST WITH KENNETH IRONS REVEALED."
HELLO?
NOW IT'LL SAY "MICROWAVE MURDERER BAKES BEAUTY #3."
A HEADLINE THE NYPD DIDN'T WANT TO SEE...

ESPECIALLY SINCE THEIR CHIEF INVESTIGATOR ON THAT SERIAL KILLER CASE, **DETECTIVE SARA PEZZINI**--
--IS CURRENTLY ACROSS THE EAST RIVER IN LONG ISLAND CITY, ENVELOPED IN **CHAOS.**
THE WALLS SHIMMER--STILL **RESONATING** WITH THE ENERGY THAT FILLED THIS HALL MINUTES AGO.
THE BODIES AROUND HER SMOLDER--**RAVAGED** BY ALIEN POWER.
IS ALL THIS POSSIBLE? IS IT SOME BIZARRE FUGUE FANTASY?
MAYBE SHE'LL WAKE UP NEXT TO YEE, IN HIS CAR. ANOTHER STAKE-OUT GONE TOO LONG. THE COFFEE MUST'VE STOPPED WORKING.
NOPE. IT HAPPENED.
ALL THIS DEVASTATION CAUSED BY...
BUT IT DIDN'T ACT **ALONE,** DID IT?

BELOW HER, THE LIFELESS FORM OF HER PARTNER, MICHAEL YEE--TORN APART BY **MAN-MADE POWER.**
...THE WITCHBLADE.
I MADE THIS HAPPEN. **ME!**
NO! I DIDN'T MEAN IT. I CAN'T BELIEVE I DID THIS...
...I...
...KILLED...
...**ALL** OF THEM...

BELLEVUE HOSPITAL.
WAIT-- I THINK SHE'S--
HEY, PEZ.
YOU'D THINK THE PARAMEDICS'D TREAT YOU **BETTER**, BEING A COP.
**SARA!**
H-HI GUYS... THERE A...(COUGH) ...PARTY OR SOMETHIN'?
YOU HAD US **WORRIED** THERE, KIDDO.
I HAD **ME** WORRIED, CHIEF...
THE DEPARTMENT REALLY WENT ALL OUT FOR YOU, PEZ--**A SEMI-PRIVATE ROOM!**
JAKE LOOKS LIKE HE'S GONNA **VOMIT.**
NO MAKE-UP. I MUST LOOK PRETTY BAD.
YEAH.
HEY--DON'T WORRY ABOUT THAT NOW, PEZ. JUST TAKE IT EASY.
HEY GUYS, IS THE FIGHT FOR JUSTICE CONTINUING WITHOUT ME?
BARELY. SELZER'S CLIMBING THE WALLS WAITING FOR YOU TO COME BACK. I HAD TO STOP HIM FROM COMING WITH! YOU KNOW THOSE L.A. GUYS.
THEY WANT TO TALK ABOUT IT SO **BADLY**--THE DEAD THUGS, THE MELTED WALLS, YEE...
HOW COULD HE **SAY THAT?** HE DIDN'T JUST SIT AND WATCH HIS PARTNER DIE!
HE DIDN'T SEE THE LINE OF **CHARRED BODIES...**
HE--

OH--YOU
OTICED THIS
THING.
YEAH, WE
UND IT AT THE
IME SCENE.
AS ON YOUR
EST WHEN WE
OT TO THE
THEATRE.
KOFF...OH, IT...UHNH...YOU KNOW...THAT'S A...KOFF... LOOK...YEE...
AHEM. I THINK IT'S TIME WE LET MISS PEZZINI, HERE, REST.
I'LL JUST LEAVE THESE-- TSK--HMPH-- GUESS I'M NOT THE ONLY ONE WHO BROUGHT FLOWERS.
C'MON, JAKE.
SEE YOU TOMORROW, SARA.

YOUR DETECTIVE IN THERE HAS ONE IMPRESSIVE CONSTITUTION, LIEUTENANT.
PUNCTURE WOUNDS OF THAT SEVERITY USUALLY TAKE MONTHS TO HEAL, BUT SHE'S ALREADY WELL ON HER WAY!
IF SHE PRACTICES SOME SORT OF HOLISTIC DISCIPLINE, I MAY HAVE TO RETHINK MY OPINIONS ON THE SUBJECT.
BUT THAT BIG VASE OF FLOWERS. I MEAN, IS THAT DANGEROUS?
MAYBE WE SHOULD GET RID OF THEM! I HEARD SOMETHING ABOUT THEM BREATHING UP ALL THE OXY--
SHE CAN HANDLE IT JAKE. LET'S GO.
BUT DO WE KNOW WHO SENT THEM?
JAKE?!?

I HATE THIS PLACE.
SMELLS LIKE DEATH.
GOTTEN MORE THAN ENOUGH WHIFFS OF THAT.
GOD I'M SCARED.
SHOULD BE DEAD.
SHOT--JUST LIKE YEE.
MICHAEL--DIDN'T HAVE THE GLOVE.
MOM? I HOPE YOU CAN HEAR ME.
I'M SORRY WE DIDN'T TALK BEFORE...
IT'S JUST...WE... I MESSED UP.
I... I...LOVE YOU.
I WISH I HAD ONE MORE CHANCE TO...TO TELL YOU.
ONE MORE CHANCE...
...TO SAVE YOU...

...SAVE YOU...
SAVE ME, PEZ? I THINK YOU BLEW THAT ONE, ALREADY.
DON'T YAAGGHH!
YOU THINK YOU CAN SAVE MY MOM, SARA?
I DON'T.
MICHAEL, LISA--IT'S DIFFERENT NOW!
LOOK AT ME! I CONTROL--
--WE CONTROL--
THE POWER OF GOD LIES IN OUR HANDS.
THE POWER OF DEATH!
THE POWER OF LIFE!
WE CAN GIVE YOU LIFE!

AND, SEVERAL HOURS LATER...
WELL. WELL-- LET'S SEE WHO SENT THIS EXPENSIVE ARRANGEMENT.
AAAH! WE--CAN-- HNHH--I--
...GASP...SORRY --NOSY ME--JUST WANTED TO KNOW WHO YOUR ADMIRER WAS. YOU ALL RIGHT?
H-HNH-- HOW LONG HAVE I BEEN OUT?
18 HOURS... OOOH...KENNETH IRONS?!? YOU GOT FRIENDS IN HIGH PLACES!
18--CAN-- CAN YOU GET ME SOMETHING TO EAT? BEEN A WHILE, YOU KNOW.
I'LL SEE WHAT I CAN DO, HON. BUT WHEN I GET BACK, YOU BETTER LIE BACK DOWN...AND TELL ME ABOUT HOW YA KNOW THAT HUNK!
GOTTA DO SOMETHING.
I GOTTA GET OUT OF HERE.

MEANWHILE, UPTOWN. AT CENTRAL PARK'S FAMOUS RESTAURANT.
A VALET TAKES A HUNDRED-DOLLAR BILL AND WAVES THIS CAR IN.
INSIDE, THOSE WHO ARE WEALTHY AND NOTORIOUS CAN GET IN WITH ADVANCE RESERVATIONS. EVERYONE ELSE IS TURNED AWAY.
AS USUAL, THE EVENING TALK IS EITHER ON BUSINESS OR SLEAZE.
FINE SPIRITS LOOSEN THE INHIBITED TONGUE.
(HEE,HEE) IF YOU SAY NO, I'LL JUST GO HOME WITH ONE OF THEM!
BACK OUTSIDE, ANOTHER CAR APPROACHES, AND A MAN EMERGES WHO HAS NO RESERVATION--DOESN'T NEED ONE. HE'S NOT GOING TO EAT OR TALK THE TRASH.
AND TO THINK I WAS SUPPOSED TO BE IN BAGHDAD, THIS EVENING.
NOTTINGHAM, IN FIVE MINUTES, HAND MY CARD TO CINDY.
OF COURSE, SIR.
IF YOU DON'T MIND ME SAYIN' SO, YOU'RE IN PRETTY GOOD SHAPE FOR A GUY THAT LOST MOST OF HIS MEN LAST NIGHT, MR. IRONS.
I MEAN, YOU TWO ARE THE ONLY ONES WHO SURVIVED THE TOURNAMENT. OH--AND THAT COP, TOO.
AND IRONS' PEOPLE WEREN'T THE ONLY LIVES LOST WHEN THE WITCHBLADE PLANTED ITSELF ON ITS NEW OWNER.

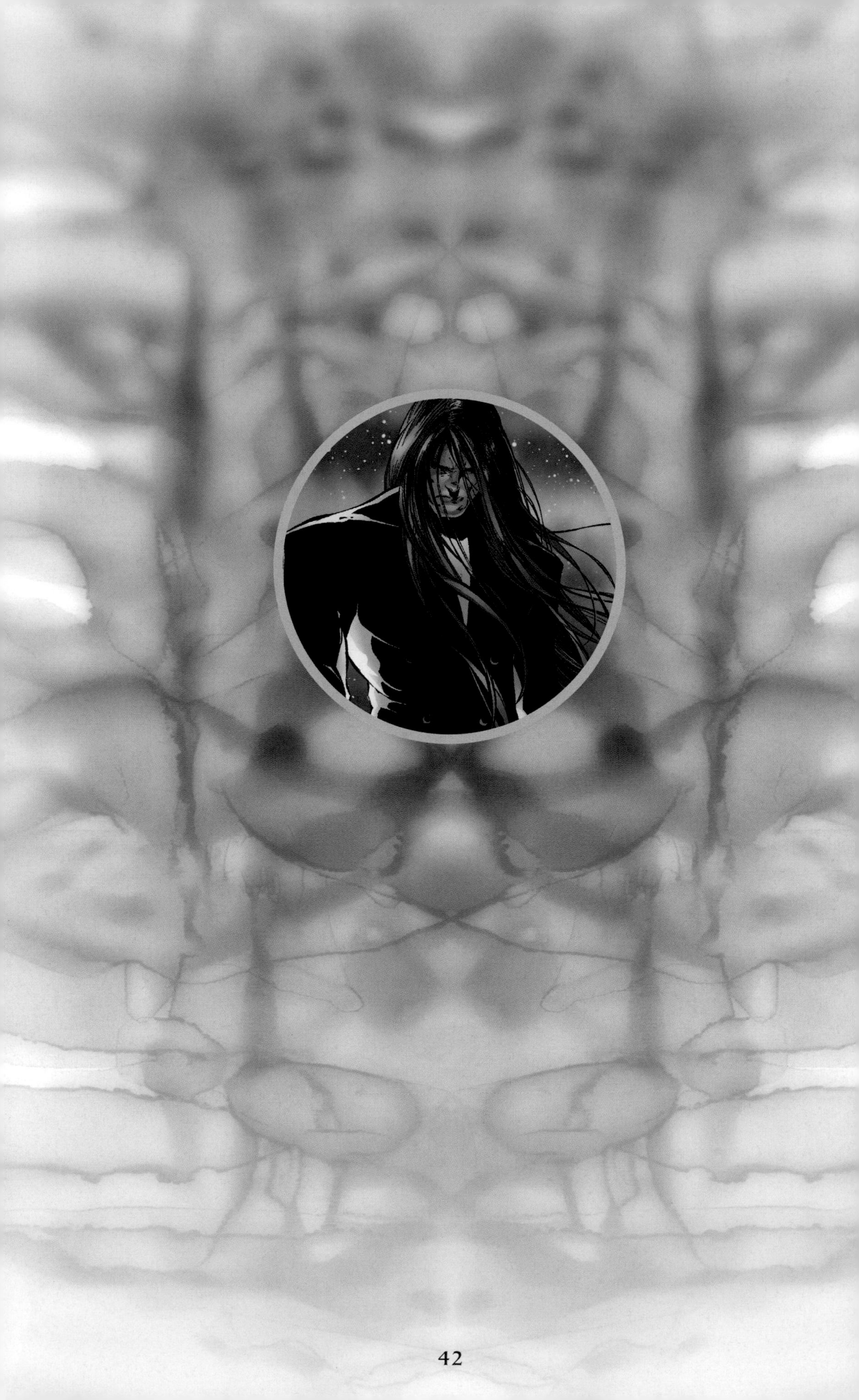

REPRESENTATIVES OF MANY CRIME FAMILIES WERE THERE.
THE FIRST TO SHOW THEIR DISPLEASURE, THE INFAMOUS TRIADS OF HONG KONG.
NONE VERY PLEASED WITH THE OUTCOME OF LAST NIGHT'S FESTIVITIES.
MR. WRIGHT, LAST NIGHT WAS A SUCCESS.
I NOW HAVE THE OPPORTUNITY TO HIRE NEW TALENTED YOUNG "CLEANERS" LIKE YOURSELF.
AND I'M CLOSER THAN I'VE EVER BEEN TO ATTAINING MY GREATEST AMBITION...
THHMMP!
YOU MAY RETALIATE NOW, NOTTINGHAM.
AI-HONG TONG, THE RIAD'S TOP ASSASSIN, AS INTERNATIONALLY NOWN FOR HIS RAZEN HITS.
HOOT THEM BETWEEN E EYES AND WALK AY--HIS TRADEMARK.
NOBODY'S EVER CAUGHT ONE OF HIS BULLETS BEFORE.
YES, SIR.
PLINK!

AN EMPIRE BUILDER LIKE IRONS ONLY SURROUNDS HIMSELF WITH SUPERIOR PEOPLE.
NO HUMAN ASSASSIN CAN TOUCH HIM.
HE THOUGHT HIS REPUTATION SPOKE FOR ITSELF.
NOT TO THE TRIADS.
THEY NEEDED PROOF.
THEY GOT PROOF.

IN THE FORM OF
IAN NOTTINGHAM.
KENNETH IRONS'
NUMBER ONE MAN.
THE ONLY MAN IRONS EVER
MET WHO SURPASSED ALL HIS
STRINGENT SPECIFICATIONS:
LOYALTY.
AGILITY.

CRUELTY.
THESE TRAITS, AND MULTITUDES OF OTHERS, HAVE WON NOTTINGHAM A PERMANENT POSITION AT IRONS INTERNATIONAL.

AND IN EXCHANGE FOR HIS SERVITUDE, ALL NOTTINGHAM ASKS FOR (BESIDES A HIGH-SEVEN-FIGURE SALARY AND ACCESS TO IRONS' VAST LASER DISC COLLECTION), IS A CHANCE TO CUT LOOSE ONCE IN A WHILE.
FOR ALTHOUGH HE RARELY DISPLAYS IT, NOTTINGHAM ENJOYS BEING THE SHOWMAN.
AND IF YOU ASK ANYONE WHO WITNESSED THE EVENTS THAT NIGHT AT THE TAVERN ON THE GREEN, THEY'D TELL YOU IT WAS SOME SHOW!

HOME.
DAMN--TOO MANY STAIRS!
LISA. BEEN HERE A WHILE.
HEY, KIDDO.
M-MOM?
AND SOON...
SARA, THERE'S THIS GUY AT SCHOOL WHO REALLY LIKES ME. BUT HE WANTS TO--YOU KNOW.
MY MOM NEVER GOT AROUND TO TEACHING ME THOSE THINGS. I JUST WISH SHE WAS ALIVE.
SHE'S TRYING SO HARD NOT TO CRY.
WELL, KIDDO, THERE'S A LOT TO LEARN ABOUT BOYS. I'M SURE THERE'S AT LEAST ONE GOOD EXAMPLE ON THIS MACHINE.
HEY, IT'S DOUG. REMEMBER ME? WE WERE SUPPOSED TO MEET AT VAZAC'S TONIGHT. GUESS YOU FLAKED AGAIN! OH, WELL. LATER.
THAT'S ME--FLAKE.
HI, SARA. IT'S JANET YEE. MICHAEL TOLD ME YOU GUYS HAD TO INVESTIGATE A CRIME SCENE, BUT I FIGURED HE'D BE HOME BY NOW.
I WAS HOPING SHE WOULDN'T SAY THAT.
ANYWAY, IF YOU GET THIS MESSAGE, CAN YOU REMIND HIM TO BRING HOME, HEHEHE, BEN AND JERRY'S ENGLISH TOFFEE CRUNCH? YOU KNOW--IMPORTANT STUFF. HOPE ALL'S WELL WITH YOU. THANKS.
GOD.
I'M SORRY, JANET.
I'M SORRY, LISA.
SORRY.
IT'S NOT OVER.

ONLY A COUPLE OF HOURS LATER...
AAAGH-- WE--CAN!
ENOUGH!

SOON...
I'LL--HOLD IT. YOU WERE RIGHT. SHE'S HERE.

DETECTIVE PEZZINI, WELCOME BACK.
FREAK. HERE AT 2 A.M. NICE LIFE.

HOW DO YOU FEEL? ANYTHING I CAN DO FOR YOU?
YEAH. HOLD THIS.
SURE!
WHEN YOU GET A CHANCE, CAN YOU TELL ME ABOUT THAT STRANGE GLOVE WE FOUND ALONGSIDE YOU? IT'S ALREADY OVER IN EVIDENCE ROOM C.
HE'S TOO CREEPY.
YEAH. LATER.

EVIDENCE
C

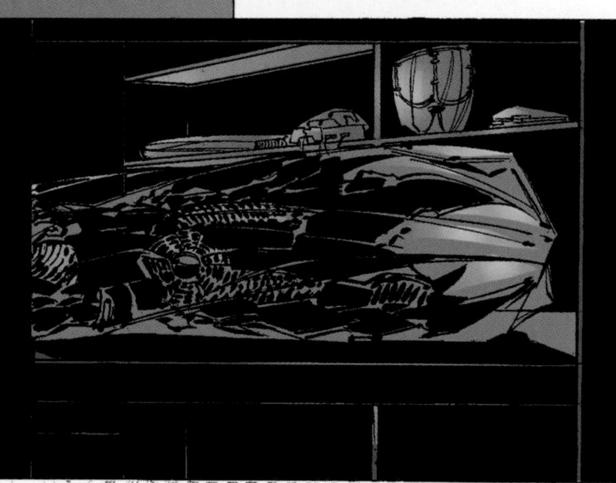

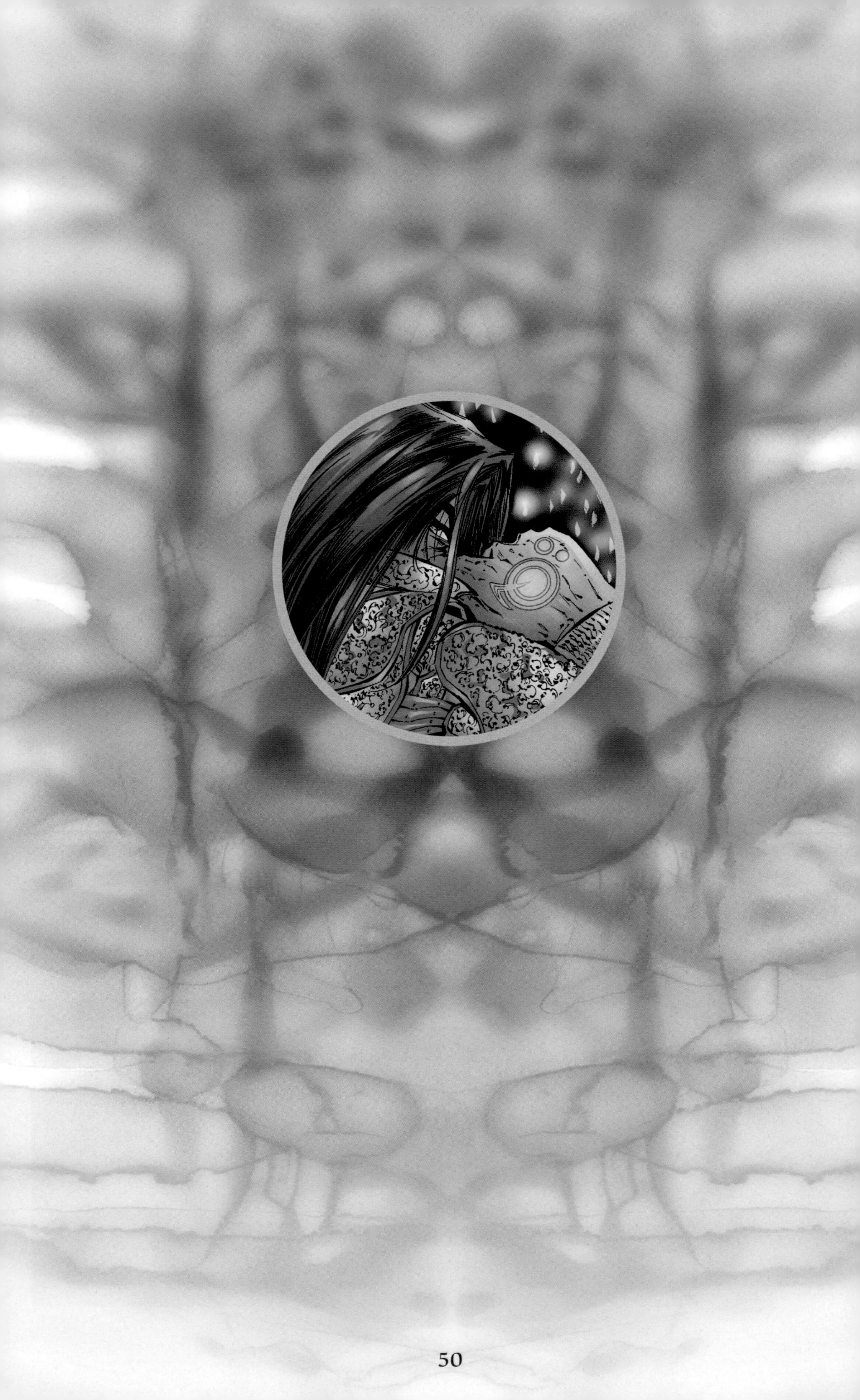

CENTRAL PARK WEST, WHERE THE PENTHOUSE GETS IT OWN SECURED ELEVATOR.
HE'S PREPARED HIS WHOLE LIFE FOR THIS DAY. IT WAS FOR THIS RITUAL THAT HE TOOK NOTTINGHAM INTO HIS EMPLOY IN THE FIRST PLACE.

TIME FOR ANOTHER BRANDING --BUT THIS ONE'S VERY DIFFERENT FROM THE OTHERS.

AT THAT PRECISE MOMENT.
CHUN
YEE, M
SEE YA, JAY. I'LL JUST LEAVE OUT THE EMERGENCY EXIT, OKAY?

THAT LYSOL SMELL!
I MUST BE LOSING MY MIND. BUT I GOTTA TRY.

AN HOUR INTO THIS HEINOUS CEREMONY, NOTTINGHAM CAN **BARELY** STAND.

SILENTLY SUPPLICANT, HE KNOWS THE WORSE IS YET TO COME.

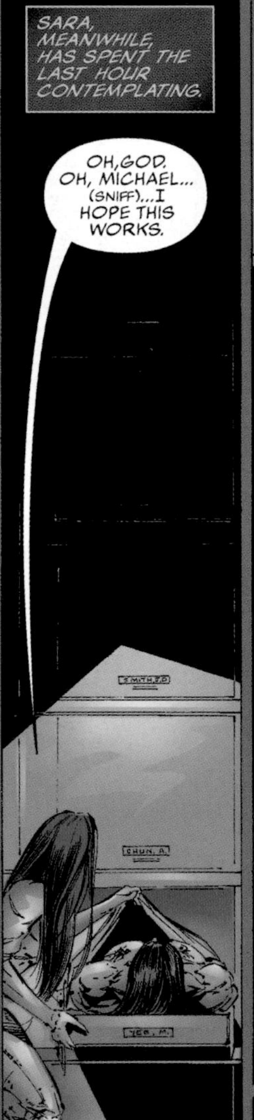

SARA, MEANWHILE, HAS SPENT THE LAST HOUR CONTEMPLATING.
OH, GOD. OH, MICHAEL... (SNIFF)...I HOPE THIS WORKS.

THE BRANDING IS INSTRUMENTAL IN THE NEUTRALIZATION OF THE WITCHBLADE. THE RUNE CARVED INTO THE HAND, IDENTICAL TO THE ONE ON THE SWORD.
IT IS WRITTEN THAT WHEN THE TWO RUNES TOUCH, THE BEARER SHALL BECOME A CONDUIT FOR THE WITCHBLADE'S TREMENDOUS ENERGIES.

I DON'T EVEN KNOW WHAT I'M SUPPOSED TO DO WITH THIS THING!
THE KNIFE GOES IN EASILY, YET NOT PAINLESSLY.
PUSHING AND SCRAPING UNTIL HE DAMAGES NERVES AND HITS BONE, IRONS CARVES THE RUNE.
UM...DEAR LORD...ER, ALMIGHTY THING, PLEASE BRING BACK MICHAEL YEE... AND...I PROMISE TO REPAY YOU.
P-PLEASE WORK. HE HAS A WIFE...(SNIFF)... AND, AND I LOVE HIM!
SHUDDERING AND BREATHLESS, NOTTINGHAM REALIZES THE BRANDING IS FINALLY COMPLETE.

I AM READY, MASTER.

FOR AN INSTANT, SARA THINKS JUST HOW SILLY SHE'D LOOK IF SOMEONE WALKED IN.
WHAT AM I DOING???
I GUESS I CAN'T DO ***ANYTHING*** RIGHT!

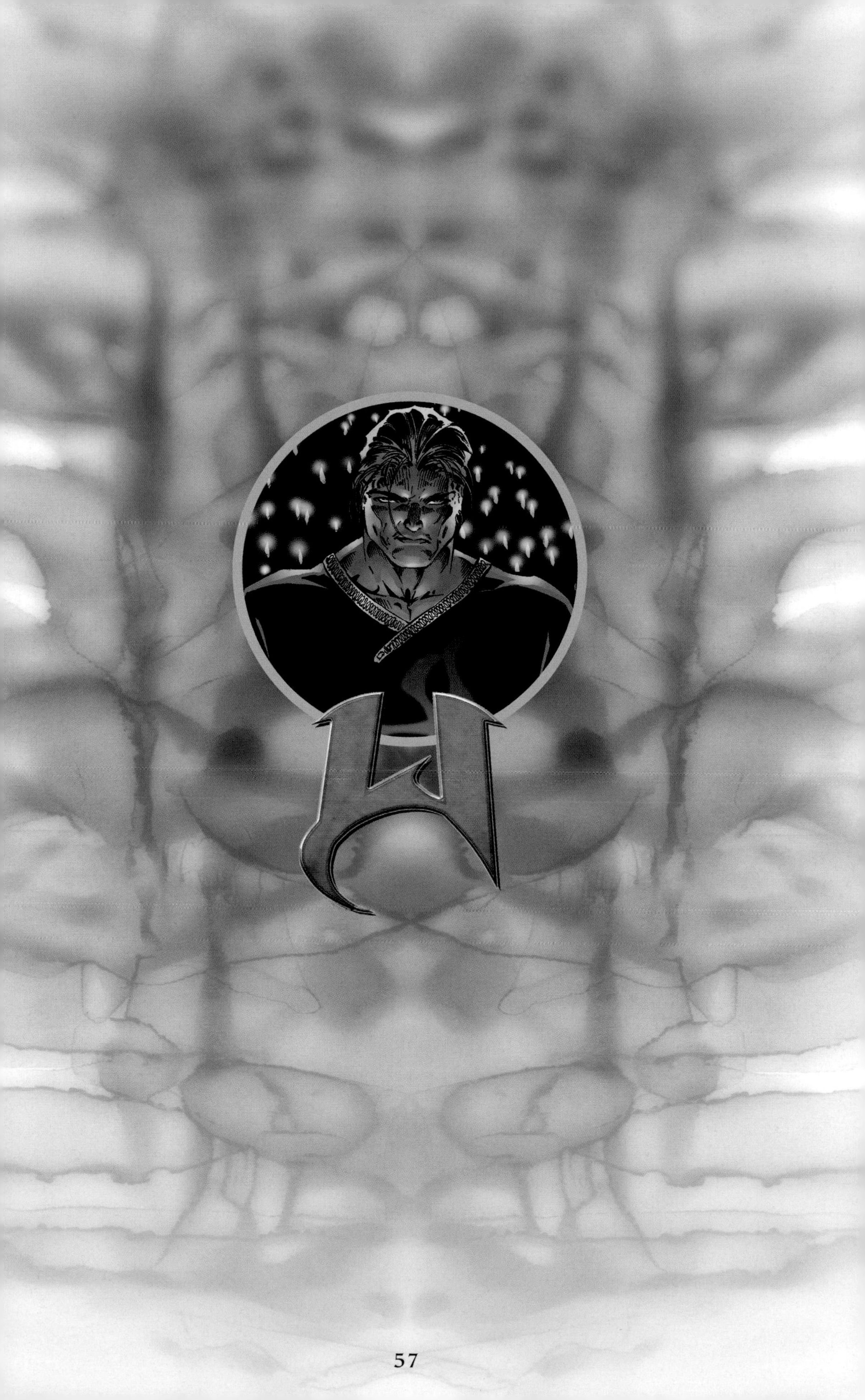

## issue #3

story: **David Wohl** and **Christina Z.**
pencils and co-plot: **Michael Turner**
inks: **D-Tron**
colors: **JD Smith**

CITY MORGUE, 3:50 A.M.
GOD, I KNOW YOU'RE PROBABLY NOT LISTENING, BUT CAN YOU ANSWER ONE QUESTION?
WHAT THE HELL WAS I THINKING?
SO I HAVEN'T THOUGHT ABOUT YOU FOR A FEW YEARS--
YOU COULD'VE SENT SOME ANGEL DOWN TO SLAP ME AND TELL ME I WAS AN IDIOT.
OH, MICHAEL--I TRIED. I THOUGHT I COULD BRING YOU BACK.
I REALLY DID.
NO MIRACLES TODAY.
HERE I WAS, THINKING I'M SARA ALMIGHTY...
NOPE. JUST PEZZINI, NYPD.
WITH HER TRUSTY SIDEKICK, THE HOLY GLOVE.
JESUS, THIS IS SICK.
WHAT THE HELL WAS I THINKING???

NEXT TIME I GET AN URGE LIKE THAT, I'M GONNA CHECK MYSELF INTO COUNTY--
N-NO...
THIS CAN'T BE--NO--
THIS ISN'T HAPPENING.
PUULGRG...
I--I--
THIS ISN'T REAL. THE FORMALDEHYDE--I'M HALLUCINATING. I'M--I'M--
MUST-- MU--
MICHAEL?
MICHAEL! YOU'RE ALIVE!

--OH--
(SNIFF) DON'T DO THAT AGAIN!
YOU'RE (SNIFF)--
NEXT TIME CALL FOR BACK-UP, OKAY?
OHH... (SNIFF)...I CAN'T WAIT TO--
HEART'S NOT BEATING.
YOU'RE SO COLD. I SHOULD KEEP YOU COVERED.
NO-- IT'S THIS ROOM--WE GOTTA--
--GET--
...KILL...
C'MON, LET'S GET YOU--
...KILL... ME...
I KNOW-- I-IT'S THIS PLACE!
I'M GONNA PULL THE CAR AROUND. JUST REST AND WE'LL GET YOU HOME.
THERE'S NO PULSE. HE'S ALIVE, BUT NOT REALLY. WHAT DID THIS THING DO TO HIM?

KILL HIM?
I--
--WE--
WHU?
NO!
YOU CAN'T! YOU CAN'T!
NOT--
--AGAIN.
4:20 A.M.
THAT'S IT!
I'VE HAD ENOUGH OF YOUR POISON TOUCH--
THIS THING'S...
--YOUR SICK THOUGHTS--
...NOT COMING OFF.
--YOUR AIMLESS THRILLS.
WHATEVER YOU ARE...
...GO TO HELL!
CREMATORIUM

8:20 A.M.
HEY, PEZ. WAKE UP! YOU'RE HOME!
C'MON. I GOTTA TAKE MY WIFE TA WORK!
URMM... THANKS, MAX.
LEFT THE HEAT ON AGAIN. CON ED'S GONNA LOVE ME THIS MONTH.
THAT'S ME. CAN'T TURN THE RADIATOR OFF, CAN'T RAISE THE DEAD.
DAMMIT! WHAT WAS THAT THING?
I WAS SHOT. SHOT! AND THE WOUNDS ARE ALREADY HEALED!
ALL THAT'S LEFT ON ME NOW ARE SOME SCRATCHES FROM WHEN I TRIED TO PULL THE DAMNED THING OFF. A LITTLE PARTING GIFT.
ARA PEZZINI--YOU UST WON THE SUPER-ERO FOR A DAY ONTEST. GOOD JOB.
NEXT TIME I'LL SEE WHAT'S BEHIND DOOR NUMBER TWO.
KNOCK! KNOCK!
NOW WHAT?!?

HEY, SARA-- I SAW IT ON THE NEWS. WHY DIDN'T YOU TELL ME YOU GOT THE GUY THAT KILLED MOM-- GALLO?
THAT'S GREAT!
SORRY. I CAN'T.
CAN I COME IN?
I WAS WONDERIN' IF YOU'D GO TO THE MINISTRY SHOW TONIGHT. TO CELEBRATE.
AH, SARA, C'MON. YOU'RE THE ONE WHO TOLD ME ABOUT THEM IN THE FIRST PLACE! YOU GOT A HOT DATE?
HEYYY! THERE SHE IS! OUR WOUNDED POLICE WOMAN.
I DIDN'T KNOW YOU CHECKED OUT OF THE HOSPITAL...WHILE YOU WERE OUT LAZING AROUND, OUR SERIAL KILLER STRUCK AGAIN, AT A GIRL BAR CALLED...(HEHE)...THE HONEY POT!
WAIT. WHAT'S THIS ABOUT A HOT DATE?
OH--I DIDN'T KNOW I HAD TO RUN MY WHOLE FREAKIN' AGENDA BY YOU, JAKE!
HEY, PEZ, I'M SORR--
SAVE IT, JAKE!
DEFINITELY NOT A MORNING PERSON!
SLAM!

BETTER BODIES, NYC.
GOOD--'CAUSE RIGHT NOW, I'D SLUG ANYONE WHO TRIED.
AARGHH--THEY'LL PROBABLY WANT ME TO SEE THE BEREAVEMENT COUNSELOR. FAT CHANCE!
GOTTA GET STRONG. CAN'T CRACK.
NO NEON, NO JUICE BAR, NO PICK-UP LINES.
CAN'T LET 'EM GET TO ME.
CAN'T LET ANYONE GET TO ME.

WHY WON'T THEY ALL JUST LEAVE ME...
...ALONE.
NO CHEAP LINE. THIS IS NEW.
SCREW IT.
NO OFFENSE, BUT GET OUTTA HERE, OKAY? I'M NOT IN THE MOOD. GO BOTHER SOMEONE ELSE!
I'M NOT HERE TO PICK ANYONE UP. NOT MY STYLE. YOU JUST LOOKED TROUBLED.
I CAN SEE IT IN YOUR FACE.
SOMETIMES SILENT COMPANY IS MORE HEALING THAN WORDS OF ADVICE. EVIDENTLY NOT IN YOUR CASE. MY MISTAKE.
BUT I KNOW WHAT IT'S LIKE FOR PEOPLE NOT TO UNDERSTAND WHAT YOU'RE GOING THROUGH.
I'VE BEEN THERE.
ANGER MANAGES EVERYTHING POORLY AND SELF PITY IS A WASTE OF TIME.
I'M SORRY, THAT WAS RUDE OF ME. I'M SARA.
DO...YOU WANT TO GO GRAB A COFFEE OR SOMETHING?
NO,
BUT GIVE ME A CALL SOMETIME. COFFEE. MY TREAT.

NEVER GOT ADVICE LIKE THAT AT BETTER BODIES BEFORE...
HMM...NEVER GOT ADVICE LIKE THAT, PERIOD!
WELL...KEN...I MAY JUST TAKE YOU UP ON THAT COFFEE.
GOTTA TELL LISA. GUESS I HAVE A "HOT DATE" AFTER ALL.
HE'S RIGHT. SELF PITY'S A WASTE OF TIME.
I CAN'T CHANGE THE PAST, BUT I CAN LET IT GO.
OH, NO. LISA. I WAS SUCH A BI--
EXCUSE ME, UH, MISS, BUT YOU KNOW WHERE I CAN FIND A PHONE 'ROUND HERE?
YOU DON'T HAVE ONE IN THAT THING?
YOU GOT...
THIS IS WRONG.
...RIPPED OFF.
HEH. YEAH, GUESS SO. WHATEVER.

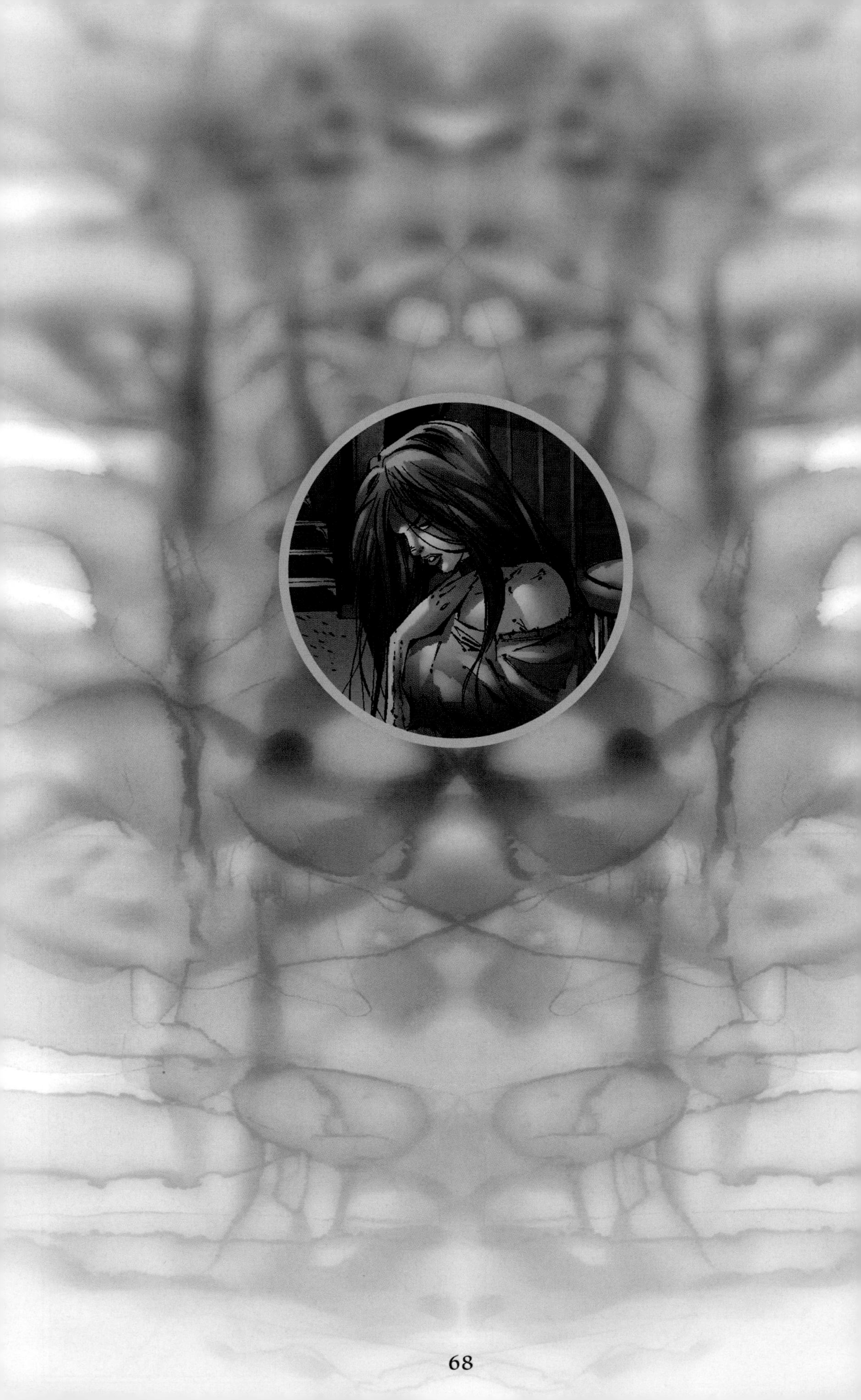

VERY WRONG.
MMM... NEVER MIND, DOLL.
I'VE SEEN THIS ACT PLAY OUT ALREADY.
CHEEZY DRESSED CREEPS WITH GUNS AND GOATEES COME TO MAKE A HIT. IN A LIMO.
AND THEY DON'T CARE WHO ELSE THEY TAKE DOWN IN THE PROCESS.
HERE ON A CROWDED STREET. THEY'RE NOT EVEN NOBLE ABOUT IT.
LISA'S MOM GOT HIT BY A STRAY BULLET...
MAYBE WE SHOULD TAKE THIS--
WOOOUUFF...
--INSIDE.
GOTTA GET AWAY FROM ALL THESE PEOPLE.
I'LL TURN INTO AN ALLEY-- GIVE 'EM A CLEANER SHOT--
--THEN MAYBE FIND OUT WHY THEY'RE AFT--
KZZZZTTTTT!
NOT...
...AGAIN...

5:44 P.M.

ALTHOUGH CALIFORNIA IS THE LAND OF THE SETTING SUN, IT GETS SOME COMPETITION FROM THE ISLE OF **MANHATTAN.**

SURROUNDED BY WATER AND FILLED WITH GLASS AND STEEL, MANHATTAN **EMBRACES** THE SUNSET, **COALESCING** WITH IT FOR A **FLEETING, RADIANT** MOMENT.

IT ALMOST MAKES YOU FORGET WHERE YOU ARE.

OVER IN BATTERY PARK, A YOUNG ART STUDENT NAMED MONICA GOT SO LOST IN THE SUNSET, SHE DIDN'T NOTICE HOW MUCH **DOPE** SHE WAS SHOOTING INTO HERSELF. TONIGHT THE COPS'LL CALL IT JUST ANOTHER DUMB **O.D.**

MEANWHILE, IN LITTLE ITALY, MOBSTER VINCENT DIBENEDETTO TOOK A MOMENT TO ENJOY THE WANING LIGHT. JUST ENOUGH TIME FOR A GAMBINO HITMAN TO **ASSASSINATE** HIM AS HE TOOK A BITE OF GNOCCI.

A FEW WEEKS AGO, ON THIS VERY SHIP, AN ACCOUNTANT OF KENNETH IRONS, EDDIE ROTH, WAS DRINKING A MARTINI AND ADMIRING THE VIEW UNTIL IRONS NOTIFIED HIM HIS SERVICES WERE NO LONGER NEEDED.

THE BODY HASN'T WASHED UP ON **SHORE,** YET.

WELL, SWEETNESS, TIME TO SLIP INTO SOMETHING MORE COMFORTABLE.
PARDON THE "CHOKER," BUT WILLIAM OVER THERE THINKS YOU'RE A SAVAGE BEAST.
IT LOOKS NICE ON YA, THOUGH.
YOU'RE LUCKY I DON'T HAVE YOU TENDING TO HIS WOUNDS. YOU CRUSHED A COUPLE OF IMPORTANT THINGS--IF YA KNOW WHAT I MEAN?
MR. WRIGHT, CAN'T WE HAVE SOME FUN WIT' HER FIRST?
MMMM... GOOD IDEA, BUT NO.
THIS IS BUSINESS.
GUESS I'M NOT GETTING THAT COFFEE ANY TIME SOON.

WHO ARE THESE--NO-- I GOT RID OF THAT THING!
I THINK YOU DROPPED THIS.
DON'T KNOW WHAT IT IS?
BUT I HEAR YOU DO.
PUT IT ON.
NO.

MAYBE I'M NOT MAKING MYSELF CLEAR.
YOU LIKE THE FEEL OF A .45 AGAINST YOUR SKULL?
WHY ARE YOU SHAKING? ARE YOU AFRAID...OR EXCITED?
DON'T FLATTER YOURSELF.
PUT IT ON.
GO TO HELL.
OH. I'M SORRY. AM I BOTHERING YOU WITH MY SILLY REQUESTS?
REALLY. THIS IS SUCH AN INCONVENIENCE FOR YOU, ISN'T IT?
NO MORE GAMES, BITCH.
BLAM!

NOW, BE A DOLL AND PUT IT ON.
YOU'RE GONNA DIE.
PROMISES, PROMISES.
YA KNOW, I'VE DEALT WITH YOUR KIND BEFORE.
YOU'RE ONE OF THOSE COPS WHO LIKES TO GET SHOT. MAKES YA THINK YOU'RE A HERO.
WELL, HERE'S A PRESENT.
PAM!
SORRY YOU'LL HAVE TO BLEED TO DEATH.
TOO BAD--YOU WERE PRETTY HOT.
IF IT WEREN'T FOR THE SEARING PAIN, SARA WOULD PROBABLY LAUGH AT HER IRONIC PREDICAMENT.

DIE, OR WEAR IT AGAIN.
LTHOUGH SHE CURRENTLY REFERS THE FORMER...
...THE WITCHBLADE DOESN'T.

HOLY--
WHAT THE HELL--
OHMIGOD!
WE'RE ALIVE...

DESTROY...
WHOA!
OOOHH...
...THEM.
...MY... HEAD...
JUST SHUT UP AND GET HER!
DESTR--
--NO. I GOTTA GET OFF THIS BOAT.
STOP HER!
KERRASSHHH!
NOOOO!

UNBOUND.

FREED FROM THE CACOPHONY OF THE YELLING VOICES AND GUNFIRE ABOVE, SARA PEZZINI GLIDES.

**OBLIVIOUS** TO THE COLD AND UNFAZED BY THE HAIL OF BULLETS, SHE DESCENDS.

SHE SHOULD FEEL **NUMB**, BUT HER SENSES CASCADE.

SHE SHOULD BE **AFRAID**, NOW SHE'S NEVER BEEN MORE CONFIDENT.

SHE SHOULD BE **DEAD**, YET SHE'S NEVER BEEN MORE ALIVE.

ALIVE, THANKS TO THE **WITCHBLADE**.

IT ENDANGERED HER. IT **SAVED** HER.

AND SHE REALIZES THAT AS LONG AS SHE WEARS IT, SHE SHARES HER MIND WITH IT.

THAT WAS TROUBLE WHILE SHE WAS **FIGHTING** IT. BUT NOW, BENEATH THE CHOPPY SEAS, SHE'S STRANGELY AT PEACE WITH IT. CONNECTED TO IT.

SHE KNOWS THEY **NEED** EACH OTHER. **SYMBIOTES.**

AND FOR THE MOMENT, SHE **ACCEPTS** IT.

SORT OF.

SHE CAN'T HELP BUT THINK THAT PART OF THE NOISE BOMBARDING HER BRAIN IS THE WITCHBLADE, LAUGHING. OR **WARNING...**

DAMMIT-- JUST KILL 'ER. IF HE FINDS OUT WHAT HAPPENED--
--HE'LL HAVE ALL YOUR ASSES! HURRY!
COMING AFTER ME NOW.
US...
I'LL STILL TAKE MY CHANCES WITH HER BEFORE I FACE MR. NOTTINGHAM.
OUR ASSES?!? HE'S THE ONE THAT DIDN'T WAIT.
MAN, TOLD YOU WE SHOULDN'T'VE GOTTEN INVOLVED IN THIS.
WE CAN...
...DO MORE...
I KNOW--WE --WE--WHATEVER YOU ARE, I CAN HEAR YOU!
LOOK-- JUST GET HER ATTENTION. I'LL TAKE HER OUT.
ALL I HEAR IS YOU!
YOU'RE DRIVING ME CRAZY!
BUT RIGHT NOW, MAYBE WE COULD WORK TOGETHER.

H-HOLD IT RIGHT THERE!
NOW WHAT?
SHOOT HER, YOU IDIOT!
OOOOOKAY-- HERE WE ARE.
WE ARE...
SO, DO SOMETH--
GASP
AAAGH!
THAT'S IT--I'M OUTTA HERE!
UM, THANKS.
RUN...
BUT... THEY'RE GONE
WHO--?
...NOW!

WHUP!
WHUP!
WHUP!

# ISSUE #4

story: **David Wohl** and **Christina Z.**
pencils and co-plot: **Michael Turner**
inks: **D-Tron**
colors: **JD Smith**

NEW YORK CITY 7:14 P.M.
--P-E-Z-Z-I-N-I-- PEZZINI! LONG BROWN HAIR? KICKBOXER?
SORRY, GUY. DON'T KNOW NUTHIN'.
BUT I KNOW SHE WAS HERE TODAY, SO GET OFF IT ALREADY.
LOOK--WE KNOW WHO SHE IS...BUT WE'RE NOT A DATING SERVICE. SO STOP WASTIN' OUR TIME.
WAIT, I--
--C'MON, PAL, YOU WANNA GIRL? GO OVER TA LEXINGTON AVENUE. YOU CAN BUY ALL DA WOMEN YA WANT OVER THERE!
BETTER BODIES
MET-RX
BODY ALIVE
THE THING ABOUT JAKE IS THAT WITH HIS FIVE YEARS ON THE FORCE, HE'S STILL TRYING TO GAIN THE REPUTATION AND RESPECT ON AN NYPD DETECTIVE --A DIFFICULT TASK WHEN YOU LOOK MORE LIKE JUST ANOTHER SURF KID FROM CALIFORNIA.
HEY, I WORK WITH HER! I'M A COP, AND SHE'S MISSING!
THIS IS THE LAST PLACE SHE'S KNOWN TO HAVE BEEN, SO IF YOU DON'T GIVE SOME ANSWERS, I'M GONNA HAUL ALL OF YOU INTO THE STATION AND YOU CAN SIT THERE WASTING TIME IN A VOMIT-DRENCHED CELL UNTIL WE CAN GET SOME ANSWERS. NOW, WHERE IS SHE?
WELL, GEEZ--WHY DINCHA SAY SO?
HEY? ANYBODY SEEN PEZ?
YEAH-- I SAW 'ER 'DIS MORNING, TALKIN' TO SOME GUY I AIN'T NEVER SEEN BEFORE.
BODY ALIVE
REAL WALL STREET-TYPE--GUY MUST'VE BEEN WEARING 'BOUT $1600 OF BROOKS BROTHERS GEAR. BIG TIME. THINK SHE LEFT WITH 'EM.
A YEAR AGO, WHEN HE FIRST MET PEZ HER HOT-TEMPERED NATURE IRKED HIM, BUT IT SEEMS THAT LITTLE BIT OF HER TRADEMARK SPARK IS ALL YOU NEED TO GET THE ANSWERS YOU WANT--EVEN IF THEY JUST LEAD TO MORE QUESTIONS.
DAMN, PEZ. WHAT ARE YOU GETTING YOURSELF INTO NOW...

SARA PEZZINI IS WELL AWARE OF WHERE THAT SPARK OFTEN GETS HER.
IT'S WHAT LED HER TO THE RIALTO THEATRE--TO SEE WHY ALL THE GANGSTERS IN TOWN WERE CONVERGING ON LONG ISLAND CITY.
NOW, ONLY A FEW DAYS LATER, SHE'S SEEN HER PARTNER GET KILLED, RESURRECTED AND KILLED AGAIN; SHE HERSELF HAS BEEN SHOT FOUR TIMES; AND EVERYTHING SEEMS TO BE HAPPENING BECAUSE OF THE WITCHBLADE--THIS EVER-PRESENT GLOVE THAT BOTH ENDANGERS AND SAVES HER LIFE ON A REGULAR BASIS...
...AND NOW THIS...
IN THE ACADEMY, THEY TOLD US THAT CRIMINALS WOULD TRY ANY TYPE OF INTIMIDATION TACTIC TO GET THE COPS TO FALTER. "OUTLANDISH GARB" WAS AMONG THEM.
IT USUALLY MEANT YOU WERE DEALING WITH A PSYCHO WHO WAS JUST TOO FAR OUT THERE, OR SOMEONE WHO WAS INTELLIGENT ENOUGH TO KNOW THAT EVEN COPS GET SCARED WHEN CONFRONTED WITH UNUSUAL SITUATIONS.
BUT I DIDN'T THINK THAT I'D EVER SEE SOMETHING LIKE THIS! SHOTGUN, SWITCHBLADE, .45, .38, .22, A CAMERA TRIPOD--HELL, I WAS ONCE ATTACKED WITH A TOASTER, BUT I NEVER BUSTED A DRUG DEALER OR TAKEN DOWN A MURDERER WHO CARRIED A SWORD--

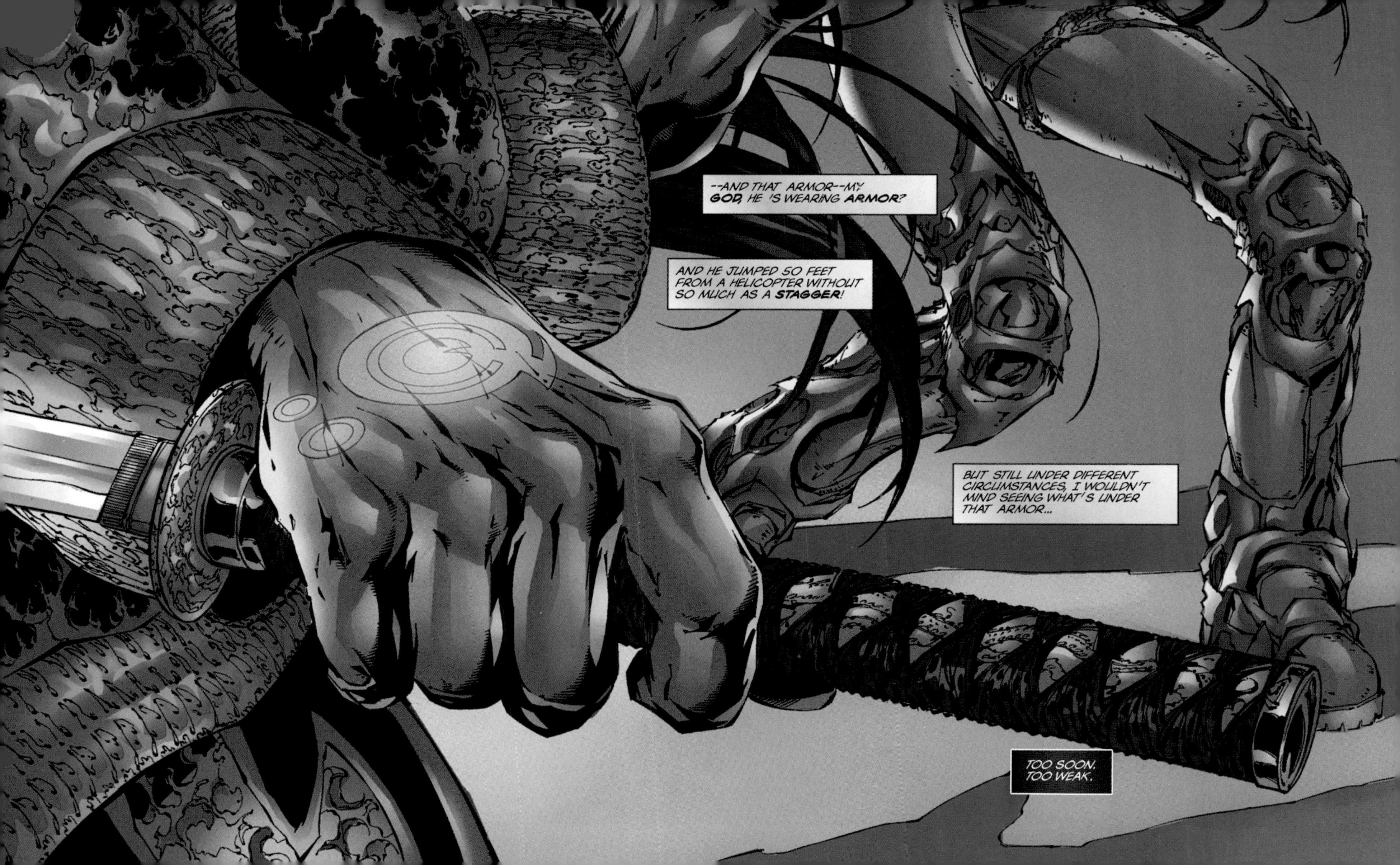
--AND THAT ARMOR--MY **GOD**, HE 'S WEARING **ARMOR**?
AND HE JUMPED 50 FEET FROM A HELICOPTER WITHOUT SO MUCH AS A **STAGGER**!
BUT STILL UNDER DIFFERENT CIRCUMSTANCES, I WOULDN'T MIND SEEING WHAT'S UNDER THAT ARMOR...
TOO SOON. TOO WEAK.

DO YOU NOT REMEMBER ME?
I DARESAY YOU ARE QUITE PROFICIENT WITH THAT GAUNTLET.
PITY YOU COULDN'T USE IT TO SAVE YOUR PARTNER'S LIFE.
IT'S IT'S...IT'S YOU!
--LEAVE!
YOU KILLED MY PARTNER... MY FRIEND.
AH--YOU DO REMEBER ME. I AM FLATTERED.
AS FOR YOUR PARTNER, PERHAPS IF HE WEREN'T SO INDISCREET, HE MIGHT STILL BE ALIVE.
INDISCREET?!? THAT S WHY YOU HAD HIM KILLED??? HE WAS A HUMAN BEING! YOU DON'T KILL A PERSON FOR BEING INDISC --
YOUR POINT BEING...?
HEAD BACK TO THE DINGHY! I'M NOT WAITIN' AROUND TO SEE HIM TAKE HER OUT, THEN US!
--LEAVE!
HIM? WHAT ABOUT HER? NONE OF THIS WAS IN WRIGHT'S CONTRACT!
AN' THAT BASTARD'S JUST WATCHIN' FROM THE YACHT!
WWHHAAMMM!
ENOUGH BANTER!

UGH! HOW COULD HE?? WHO IS HE? WHAT IS HE?
NO...
FLEE!
DON'T CARE WHAT HE IS--HE'S MINE, NOW!
LEAVE!
NO CHANCE!
I KNOW WHAT YOU CAN DO AND I KNOW WHAT I'M CAPABLE OF! I'M NOT RUNNING AWAY FROM THIS ONE!
CAN'T
YES!
NOW YOU'RE DOING WHAT I WANT...
YES.

UNLIKE SARA PEZZINI, IAN NOTTINGHAM HAS NO SPARK.
HE SMOLDE
HE'S PATIENT.
IT'S THE WAY HE GAINS CONTROL AND KEEPS IT.
HE KNOWS ABOUT SARA AND HER SPARK, AS WELL AS THE WEAPON SHE WIELDS, SO HE LETS HER TAKE THE BATTLE TO HIM, AS PER THE PLAN.
C'MON FIGHT ME, YOU BASTARD!
I'VE TAKEN ON WORSE THAN YOU--WEREN'T AS --UNGH--FINELY DECORATED-- AND--
--I BEAT THEM TOO!
DON'T...
VVVVZZZZTTTTT!

MURRAY, WHERE'D JA GO?
WHAT TH--
SIR! HIT'S GONE DIRTY! ALL HELL'S BREAKIN' LOOSE...I'M OFF THIS JOB!
BMPT!
YES, YOU ARE.
WELL, THIS SURE IS A SHAME, I'M KINDA INTO TOUGH GUYS, YOU KNOW.
VVVVZZZT!
IF HE WERE ASKED, IAN NOTTINGHAM WOULD PROBABLY ADMIT THAT FOR A MOMENT HE WAS UNSURE OF WHAT WOULD HAPPEN WHEN HE BEGAN TO ABSORB THE WITCHBLADE'S ENERGY. YES, HE WOULD ADMIT HE WAS STARTLED.
FINALLY!
NO REHEARSAL COULD'VE PREPARED HIM FOR THE INVIGORATION HE FELT.
NOTHING FEELS LIKE THE WITCHBLADE.

AND, UNFORTUNATELY, NO ONE CAN CONTROL ITS RAW POWER.
JUST LIKE ANYTHING ELSE IN LIFE-- YOU MAY HAVE THE SCHOOLING BUT IT'S THE ON-THE-JOB EXPERIENCE THAT COUNTS...
NO--STOP!
DRAINING--
I KNOW YOU INTENDED TO DO ME IN, AND I GIVE YOU FAIR CREDIT FOR **TRYING**, BUT YOU ARE **OUTCLASSED.**
YOUR WEAK EFFORTS **BEG** TO TIRE ME.
STAY BACK! I'LL-- I'LL--

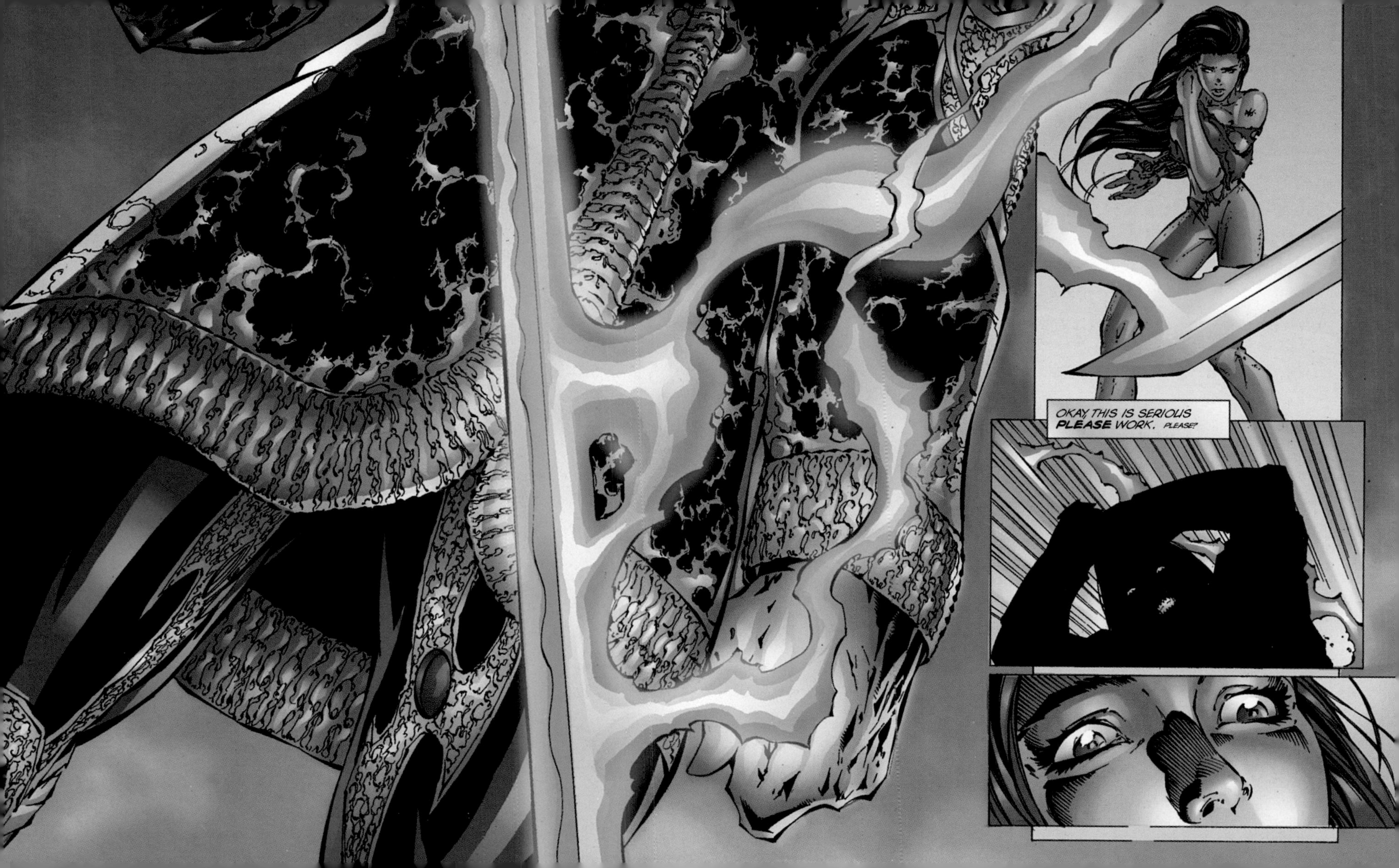
OKAY, THIS IS SERIOUS
PLEASE WORK. PLEASE?

THIS THING WON'T DEFLECT MANY MORE BLOWS--NO USE IN WAITING AROUND TO GET WHALED ON.
KANK!
UNGH!
AH, A LITTLE TOO CONFIDENT, EH, MS. PEZZINI.
BUT YOU SIMPLY HAVE THAT INNOCENT, LOST LOOK THAT--
--INVITES ABUSE!
YOU'RE HELLISHLY DETERMINED, AREN'T YOU? YOUR GAUNTLET WON'T WORK FOR YOU NOW, OR HAVEN'T YOU REALIZED THAT YET?
YOU'VE SUCH A BEAUTIFUL NECK. DEAR GIRL, DON'T LOOK SO FRIGHTENED--
--BREAKING IT WOULD BE TOO FAR OF AN EASY DEATH FOR YOU. I INTEND TO MAKE YOU SUFFER FIRST, THEN KILL YOU.

MEANWHILE AT THE STATION...
--PEZ FORWARDED ALL THE INFO TO JAKE. ALSO, CHECK WITH FORENSICS.
'SCUSE ME?
HEY, LOOKS LIKE FIELD TRIP DAY.
SORRY, KID, WE DON'T DO TOURS OF THE HOMICIDE DEPARTMENT.
NO, I'M LOOKING FOR SARA PEZZINI.
WELL, SPEAK OF THE DEVIL. SORRY, SARA'S RECOUPING. SHE, HMM...GOT "INJURED" ON THE JOB--SHE'S PROBABLY AT HOME, RESTING.
INJURED? BUT I SAW HER THIS MORNING AND SHE LOOKED OKAY--
WELL, WELL. ALL THESE QUESTIONS. THANK YOU, GENTLEMEN, I'LL HANDLE THIS.
SO YOU'RE LOOKING FOR SARA PEZZINI?
UM-UM-I WAS--
YOU. I KNOW YOU. YOU'RE THE GIRL IN THAT MILK COMMERCIAL WITH ALL THE MODELS.
UM-YEAH.
WELL, WELL. A MODEL.
SELZER! DO YOU REALLY HAVE THE TIME TO CHIT-CHAT WITH VISITORS? I'M STILL WAITING FOR YOUR REPORT!
HOW CAN I HELP YOU, LISA?
UH, I GOTTA GO. THANKS ANYWAY.

LAST TIME I WAS ON LIBERTY ISLAND WAS WHEN I WAS IN **SIXTH GRADE.** CLASS TRIP.

DIDN'T WANT TO GO. THOUGHT THE PLACE WAS ONLY FOR **GEEKS** AND **TOURISTS**.

BUT IT WAS A WAY TO GET OUT OF THE CITY FOR A DAY. GET SOME NEW SIGHTS AND SOUNDS BESIDES HORNS BLARING AND PEOPLE SCREAMING.

AND **DAD** TOLD ME I'D APPRECIATE IT.

SO THERE I WAS, HEARING MY TEACHER, MR. COLLINS, EXPLAIN ALL THE PERTINENT FACTS OF THIS PLACE.

I STILL REMEMBER A COUPLE: 151 FEET TALL, DESIGNED BY THE GUY THAT MADE THE EIFFEL TOWER--STUFF LIKE THAT.

BUT ABOVE ALL, I REMEMBER THE **FACE.**

THE STATUE'S FACE, DESIGNED TO HAVE AN EXPRESSION THAT WOULD INSPIRE **PERSEVERANCE** IN THOSE WHO LOOKED UPON IT.

I **DO** APPRECIATE THAT.

AND I **PERSEVERE.**

I WONDER IF ALL THIS IS MY **LIFE** FLASHING BEFORE MY EYES.

IS THIS WHAT ALL MURDER VICTIMS THINK ABOUT AS THEY LAY DYING, HOURS BEFORE THEY GET DISCOVERED BY SOME DESENSITIZED HOMICIDE DETECTIVE?

NOW I SHAL DISSECT YOU SLOWLY, UNTIL I CAN PULL YOUR ORGANS FROM YOUR BROKEN CAVITY.

**NO, DAMMIT--** I'M GONNA GET OUT OF THIS!

HUNH?
KRAK!
OOLLPH!
RUN, SARA!
WHAT ARE YOU WAITING FOR? RUN!!
*KOFF* WHO?

BLOODY HELL! I DON'T BELIEVE I'VE GOT TO COME IN AND CLEAN UP YOUR MISTAKES. I TRUSTED YOU, IAN. DID YOU NOT SEE WHAT WAS OCCURRING?
I SHOULDN'T HAVE BEEN BROUGHT INTO THIS. FIVE YEARS, WE'VE WORKED TOGETHER, I CARE FOR YOU LIKE A BROTHER, BUT--
--YOU WILL PAY FOR THIS, TOMORROW.
WHAT DO YOU SUPPOSE WOULD HAPPEN IF SHE CONNECTS ME WITH YOU? I CAN'T HAVE THAT, CAN I?
KEN???
QUICKLY, GO!
WH-WHY, ARE...
SIGH DESPITE YOUR ACTIONS TODA I KNOW I'LL NEVER FIND ANYONE LIKE YO IAN, YOU ARE INDISPENSABLE TO M PLEASE REMEMBER THAT.

OH GOD. HE WAS FOLLOWING ME! WHY?!? HOW COULD HE--?
THE DINGHY--I'VE GOT TO GET TO THE DINGHY.
PULL YOURSELF TOGETHER, PEZ. JUST RELAX. THINK FOR A SECOND.
ALL OF IT--THE RIALTO --THE KILLING--THIS GLOVE--AND--
:GASP: --KEN! WHAT THE HELL WAS--
SARA, YOU'RE SLIPPING INTO SHOCK. TAKE MY COAT. YOU NEED TO KEEP WARM. I'LL TAKE YOU TO THE HOSPITAL--YOU NEED X-RAYS.
NO. LEAVE ME ALONE. I DON'T EVEN **KNOW** YOU!
SARA, YOU'RE IN SHOCK. YOUR EYES DON'T SEE THINGS RIGHT WHEN YOU'RE IN SHOCK--
THANKS--DON'T--DON'T TOUCH ME--I HURT.
I--I GOTTA GO. DON'T FOLLOW ME.
FINE.

ELSEWHERE...
AH, YOU! YOU ARE FOLLOWING ME, NO?
FELINE, MY ONLY MYSTERY ABOUT YOU IS WHY YOU EVER DECIDED TO BECOME A DOMESTIC ANIMAL!
I SHALL BECOME MAD. YES, I KNOW. I WILL.
TAKE ME IN--LET ME INSIDE YOUR TINY BRAIN. OH PLEASE, BUT FOR A MOMENT? I SHALL TAKE THE TINIEST OF HATCHETS AND GENTLY HACK AWAY INTO YOU UNTIL I CAN SEE THROUGH YOUR EYES.
RIALTO
RIALTO
HAHAHH, OH, I KNOW YES, I AM. FOR I TOO, AM SEIZED WITH HOW BEAUTIFUL YOU REALLY ARE! RUN ALONG AND PLAY. HAPPY AS A YOUNG GOD, HE IS! SUCH FUR! I KNOW.
YES--YOU'RE RIGHT --TO THE MATTER AT HAND.

THIS? HOW COULD I? POLICE TAPE, HMMPH! AND NO RED CARPET TO WELCOME ME.
I FELT THE CHANDELIER IN MY HEAD. EACH TINY CRYSTAL LIT LIKE A THOUSAND BURNING FLAMES HOW BRIGHT YOU ARE!
AND HERE YOU ARE. SO CLOSE I CAME, YES I KNOW. YOU ARE STILL WARM. YOU ARE STILL READY--YOU ARE READY FOR ME!!
I'M SWALLOWING YOUR TRACKS. YOU ARE NOT HERE, BUT I KNOW WHERE YOU'VE BEEN. AND SOON I WILL KNOW WHERE YOU ARE.
AND FINALLY, WE'LL BE TOGETHER AGAIN!

10:50 PM
...MAYBE. I'M WORKING ON A CASE. IT MIGHT DRAG ON A WHILE, BUT I'LL TRY TO MAKE IT OUT THERE.
...AND NEXT ON MANHATTAN CABLE 81, THE NUDE TALK SHOW--PLEASE STAY TUNED...
KNOK! KNOK!
OH, SOMEONE'S AT THE DOOR. I'LL TALK TO YOU LATER, MOM. UH-HUH, ME TOO. BYE.
SARA! HEY, I'VE BEEN LOOKING FOR--JESUS, SARA,--WHAT HAPPENED TO YOU?
WERE YOU IN AN ACCIDENT? DID SOMEONE DO THAT TO YOU? OH MY GOD, SARA, WHO HURT YOU?
JAKE, IT'S NOTHING YOU NEED TO BE CONCERNED ABOUT. I CAN HANDLE IT. CAN I JUST COME IN AND CRASH FOR A WHILE?
FINE. FORGET IT. I'M GOING.

NO, WAIT. STOP--SARA-- PLEASE COME IN.
HERE, LET ME TAKE YOUR-- MAN, WHO'S COAT IS THIS? THAT'S ONE HARDCORE TRENCH YOU GOT THERE.
JAKE, PLEASE? I WANT TO KEEP IT ON, OK?
FINE, FINE. SORRY.
SLAM!
WELL, HOLLER IF YOU NEED ANYTHING. REALLY, I MEAN ANYTHING.
OKAY--FINE--YOU DON'T HAVE TO TALK ABOUT THE BROOKS BROTHERS GUY YOU WERE HANGING OUT WITH TODAY...OR...OR...LOOK PEZ, IT'S JUST THAT I CARE FOR YOU--A LOT. OKAY...WELL...I'LL SHUT UP NOW. GOOD NIGHT.
VE SEEN ENOUGH PEOPLE IN HOCK TO KNOW THAT'S JUST HAT I'M FEELING NOW. SO MANY THINGS I SHOULD THINK BOUT.
I SHOULD BE WONDERING WHAT ELSE THIS THING CAN DO. I SHOULD BE THINKING ABOUT PUTTING ICE ON MY FACE--BUT SITTING HERE RIGHT NOW, ALL I CAN THINK ABOUT IS TRYING TO PLACE THE SCENT OF COLOGNE I SMELL FROM THIS BEAUTIFUL COAT.
I CAN'T HELP THINKING ABOUT WHO HAD THIS ON BEFORE I DID. THE ARMS--RATHER THE FISTS (OF WHICH ONE IS UNDOUBTEDLY BRUISED BY NOW)--THAT WENT THROUGH THESE VERY SLEEVES.
THE WARMTH AND HEFT OF HIS COAT SHOULD MAKE ME FEEL SAFE. I WISH IT DID.
AND FOR THE FIRST TIME IN A COUPLE OF DAYS, THE GLOVE GLIDES OFF WITHOUT A PROBLEM. SOMETHING ELSE I SHOULD PONDER INSTEAD OF THINKING ABOUT THE MAN WHO RESCUED ME THIS EVENING.
TOMORROW I'LL THINK ABOUT THINGS LIKE MY RENT, MY JOB, AND THE WHOLE MESS THAT TRANSPIRED TODAY. BUT FOR NOW, I'M GOING TO SLEEP.

3:20 A.M.
...WE INTERRUPT "MANHATTAN'S DIRTIEST HOME VIDEOS" FOR THIS SPECIAL NEWS REPORT.
...UH--AM I ON? OH--HEY--THIS IS BECCA. AS YOU KNOW, WE HERE AT CHANNEL 81 STRIVE TO BRING YOU THE NEWS THAT THE OTHER NETWORKS ARE AFRAID TO COVER, THAT'S WHY WE'RE HERE LIVE AT LIBERTY ISLAND, WITH THIS LATE-BREAKING STORY.
AS YOU CAN SEE, THERE'S JUST CHAOS HERE. THE BODIES OF THREE MEN WERE FOUND BY A FERRY TECHNICIAN.
TWO OF THE MEN WERE SHOT IN THE HEAD AND ONE MAN WAS, UH, APPARENTLY SPEARED THROUGH THE HEAD IN WHAT POLICE SEEM TO BE SPECULATING AS AN ARMS DEAL GONE BAD.
THIS REPORTER SMELLS A COVER-UP.
RUMOR HAS IT THAT BOTH THE FBI, CIA, AND NASA ARE ON HAND, INVESTIGATING A MYSTERIOUS ORGANIC ALLOY THAT WAS FOUND AT THE CRIME SCENE. SUPPOSEDLY, THE STUFF DISSOLVED WHEN TOUCHED.
WAIT-- THERE'S ONE OF THE INVESTIGATORS--
EXCUSE ME, SIR--IS IT TRUE THAT YOU GUYS FOUND SOME ALIEN SUBSTANCE, HERETOFORE UNSEEN BY HUMANS? WHAT'S THE CONNECTION BETWEEN THIS AND THE RIALTO? WE WANT ANSWERS!
WHAT THE HELL--WHAT ARE YOU DOING HERE? GET THE HELL OUT--NO COMMENT! HEY--IS THAT THING ON???
SOUNDS LIKE A COVER-UP TO ME.
SOMEONE CUT THAT THING OFF.

HEY--WHAT'RE YOU--THIS IS BECCA UNCOVERING NEWS YOU WON'T SEE ANYWHERE ELSE! OPEN YOUR EYES PEOPLE! THIS IS A CONSPIRACY
...--OPEN YOUR EYE--BBBBBZZ ZZZZZZZ

## ISSUE #5

story: **David Wohl** and **Christina Z.**
pencils and co-plot: **Michael Turner**
inks: **D-Tron**
colors: **JD Smith**

FROM AN OUTSIDER'S POINT OF VIEW, IT SEEMED SO NORMAL.
MORNING IN MANHATTAN. A GIRL SLEEPING IN A GUY'S BED. JAKE'S BED.
FUNNY. IT DID SEEM NORMAL. BUT SOMETHING VERY ABNORMAL HAPPENED WHILE I SLEPT.
I KEEP GOING OVER IT IN MY MIND. IF I TRY TO CONCENTRATE ON IT FOR VERY LONG, THE FEELING DISAPPEARS.
A FEELING I HAD WHILE I WAS SLEEPING--LIKE A DREAM IT FELT TOO REAL.
WHAT AM I SAYING? IT WAS REAL.

I FELT IT ON ME, LIKE SOME PROTECTIVE SHELL. AND THE WEIRD THING IS--IT FELT RIGHT ON ME. AND I DIDN'T WANT TO WAKE UP BECAUSE IT FELT SO GOOD. SO SAFE.
AS I LAY THERE, SLOWLY COMING OUT OF MY SLEEP, MY MIND BEGAN ITS DAILY ROUTINE OF SORTING OUT THE STUFF FROM THE PREVIOUS DAY.
AND WHAT IT SORTED WAS NEITHER NORMAL NOR SAFE.
I KNOW HOMICIDE DETECTIVES AREN'T KNOWN FOR HAVING REGULAR LIVES, BUT THIS WAS PRETTY CRAZY--EVEN BY OUR STANDARDS.
I COULD SEE MYSELF WRITING IT UP ON A STATUS REPORT.
Attempted to bring Yee, my old partner, back to life with glove that was EXHIBIT C at the Rialto disaster, threw the glove in the coroner's incinerator and proceeded to Better Bodies gym to work off some frustration...
I'D GO ON TO WRITE THAT...
While there, I met an interesting man, KEN, and upon my departure, was KIDNAPPED by high-end thugs, taken aboard a YACHT and forced to put on the glove that SOMEHOW ended up in THEIR hands.
CHIEF SIRY'D BE READING IN DISBELIEF ESPECIALLY WHEN HE CAME TO MY NOTES ABOUT...
the man wielding a BROADSWORD, who was the very person who KILLED my partner at the Rialto.
And like me, he'd be SUSPICIOUS about Ken arriving on Liberty Island at the moment of my near-demise.

AND IF YESTERDAY'S EVENTS WEREN'T ODD ENOUGH, TODAY'S WERE JUST BEGINNING!
PEZ? YOU AWAKE?
UNTIL THAT MOMENT, I HADN'T REALIZED THE GLOVE THAT I'D THROWN CARELESSLY ON THE FLOOR LAST NIGHT HAD SOMEHOW ENDED UP BACK ON MY HAND.
BUT WHEN JAKE KNOCKED ON THE DOOR WITH BREAKFAST, IT SUDDENLY FELT BULKY. ALIEN.
HE OPENED IT LIKE A FRAT GUY IN HIS DORM, NOT EVEN THINKING THAT I MIGHT BE TOTALLY NAKED. WHICH I PRETTY MUCH WAS.
GASP
AND THEN IT HAPPENED. THE GLOVE--CHANGED. BEFORE MY EYES. AS IF IT DIDN'T WANT JAKE TO SEE IT. UNLIKE ME AT THE MOMENT, IT WAS MODEST.
OH, SORRY. I'LL COME BACK.
NO, IT'S OK. COME IN.
I'LL JUST SET THIS OVER--
--HOLY-- SARA, LOOK AT YOUR FACE!
JAKE, YOU DON'T HAVE TO RUB IT IN.
NO, SARA, I MEAN IT. LOOK!
?!?
I'VE HEARD OF A QUICK RECOVERY.. SARA, WHAT HAPPENED?
I SHOULD HAVE BEEN STUMBLING OVER MY WORDS, NERVOUS, ANXIOUS, AND, MORE THAN ANYTHING, STILL BADLY BRUISED. BUT I WAS NONE OF THOSE.
OH, YOU KNOW, I'M A REAL QUICK HEALER, JAKE.
OH, JAKE, JUST LEMME EAT. I'LL BE OUT IN A FEW MINUTES.
UH, OK. TAKE YOUR TIME.

I REALIZED THAT I WASN'T EVEN HUNGRY AS MY EYES WANDERED DOWN KEN'S JACKET ON THE FLOOR.
I PICKED APART THE REASONS WHY I DECIDED NOT TO HANG IT UP LAST NIGHT-- LIKE I WAS MINIMIZING HIM IN MY MIND BY KEEPING IT ON THE FLOOR. I WAS BUGGED AT HOW A TOTAL STRANGER COULD ENTER MY PERSONAL SPACE SO QUICKLY.
THE CARD HE GAVE ME WITH HIS NUMBER ON IT IS JUST BEGGING ME TO CALL AND FIND OUT MORE ABOUT HIM. AND RIGHT NOW'S AS GOOD A TIME AS ANY TO GET STARTED...
SOME-THING'S GOING ON--
--HEY JAKE.
I UH, BORROWED SOME OF YOUR CLOTHES. SOME TASTE YOU GOT HERE, BUT I CAN SAY, I'VE WORN WORSE.
LOOK, ON A SERIOUS NOTE, I'M REALLY SORRY 'BOUT LAST NIGHT. YOU KNOW IT'S BEEN HECTIC. I REALLY DIDN'T MEAN TO IMPOSE.
SARA, YOU CAN IMPOSE ANY TIME YOU WANT.
WELL, JAKE, I MIGHT TAKE YOU UP ON THAT.
YOU DO THAT.
SARA, WE NEED TO TALK LATER, OK? IT'S ABOUT WORK.
YOU GOT IT, JAKE. SEE YA.
WHA-- BROKEN??
WHAT THE HELL IS HAPPENING?
MAMBO

NOW, IAN, I'VE CALLED THIS MEETING TO TELL YOU THAT THERE WAS **ABSOLUTELY NO EXCUSE** FOR YOUR BEHAVIOR YESTERDAY-- **NONE.** YOU **HEAR** ME? **NONE!**

I METICULOUSLY PREPARED YOU FOR THIS. I ENTRUSTED YOU WITH-- WITH A **GIFT.** A GIFT OF **POWER.** AND YOU **ABUSED** IT!

APPARENTLY, YOU WERE **TOO BUSY** USING THAT NEW-FOUND POWER TO SEE THAT YOU WERE **RUINING** MY PLAN!

WERE YOU **INTENDING** TO USE IT FOR YOUR OWN SELFISH--?

BEEP! BEEEP!

AHEM. HELLO? AH, MR. SUMNER. I'VE BEEN LOOKING FORWARD TO HEARING FROM YOU. NO, NOT BUSY AT ALL. JUST HAVING A LITTLE **STAFF MEETING.**

OH, MR. SUMNER, YOU ARE **TOO** KIND! BUT IT IS YOU WHO SHOULD BE THANKED. YOUR WORK WITH **AMNESTY INTERNATIONAL** HAS BEEN **EXEMPLARY.**

I'VE BEEN TO **MANY** COUNTRIES AND I'VE SEEN THE MULTITUDES OF **ATROCITIES** COMMITTED AGAINST **UNDESERVING** PEOPLE.

AND IF I COULD **SOMEHOW** PREVENT **ONE** PERSON FROM BEING **WRONGLY** TORTURED, THAT ALONE WOULD BE WORTH MY DONATION.

YES, LUNCH IS **PERFECT.**

HMM...MAYBE AROUND A **QUARTER MILLION.** I'LL HAVE MY CHECKBOOK READY. GOOD-BYE.

WELL, NOTTINGHAM, I HOPE YOU WILL LEARN YOUR LESSON ABOUT POWER AND HOW IT CORRUPTS.
I'M DOING THIS BECAUSE I CARE.
AND REMEMBER--IF ANYTHING LIKE THIS EVER HAPPENS AGAIN, I'LL EXPECT YOU TO CHOOSE FROM AMONG MY MORE BRUTAL METHODS OF PUNISHMENT--INSTEAD OF A MERE THOUSAND GALLONS OF WATER.
PITY, YOUR SILLY HENCHMAN, WRIGHT, COULDN'T BE HERE TO CONSOLE YOU.
PSI

10:10 A.M.
EVERYONE IN THE NEIGHBORHOOD TOLD MARIA BUZANIS THAT HER DAUGHTER, LISA, SHOULD BE A MODEL.
LISA THOUGHT IT WOULD BE COOL (WHAT 12 YEAR OLD WOULDN'T?), SO SHE AND MOM WENT TO THE COPE MODELING AGENCY TO SEE WHAT WAS AVAILABLE.
Boucher
Boucher MODELING & CASTING AGENCY
YES, WE'VE BEEN HANDLING YOUR AGENCY'S RECORDS AND ACCOUNTS FOR TWO YEARS NOW, EVER SINCE BOUCHER MODELING AND CASTING BOUGHT IT OUT.
OH, AND LISA, OUR NAME IS PRONOUNCED "BOO-SHAY", NOT "BOW-CHER". THE RECEPTIONIST GOT QUITE A KICK OUT OF THAT WHEN YOU ASKED FOR DIRECTIONS.
80% OF THE WORK AT BOUCHER IS HAUTE COUTURE--RUNWAY MODELING. ALL THE TOP DESIGNERS USE OUR GIRLS. YOU COULD SAY WE'RE THE CHANEL OF THE MODELING WORLD.
AFTER A BRIEF APPEARANCE IN A SIX FLAGS GREAT ADVENTURE COMMERCIAL, LISA LANDED THE ROLE THAT MADE HER INFAMOUS FOR ONE LONG SUMMER...
THE "MILK GIRL."
IF YOU WATCHED TV FOUR YEARS AGO, ODDS ARE YOU SAW THAT COMMERCIAL MORE THAN ENOUGH TIMES. THE ONE WHERE THIS 12-YEAR-OLD GIRL IS SURROUNDED BY MODELS AND LEARNS THAT IF SHE DRINKS MILK, SHE COULD BE LIKE THEM.
COME. I WANT TO SHOW YOU THE STUDIO WHERE THE GIRLS GET READY FOR LOCAL ASSIGNMENTS, TEST SHOTS AND MAGAZINE SHOOTS.
THERE'S A FASHION MOGUL IN TOWN FROM GERMANY. IT'S THE NEW DIE FORM LINE. TAKE A LOOK AT SOME OF THE DESIGNS...

THAT SUMMER, LISA GOT A TASTE OF THE PRICE OF FAME.
AS SOON AS THE COMMERCIAL AIRED, EVERYONE STARTED CALLING HER THE "MILK GIRL."
IT WAS FUN FOR A LITTLE WHILE, BUT WHEN CABBIES AND CONSTRUCTION WORKERS STARTED YELLIN 'YO, I GOT YER MILK RIGHT HERE!', LISA DECIDED THIS WASN'T MUCH FUN AFTER ALL, AND GAVE UP HER BURGEONING CAREER.
RECENTLY, SHE'S HAD SECOND THOUGHTS.
IF LISA HAD SOUGHT PROFESSIONAL HELP LIKE SHE WAS TOLD TO AFTER HER MOTHER'S DEATH, HER THERAPIST WOULD PROBABLY HAVE DIAGNOSED AN ATTENTION-STARVED CHILD.
LISA WOULD ARGUE THAT SHE HAS FRIENDS, AND SHE GETS SUPPORT FROM AUNT RHONDA, WHO CURRENTLY TAKES CARE OF HER, AS WELL AS HER FRIEND, SARA PEZZINI.
NOW COME ON, THIS IS FOR BELLISIMA MAGAZINE. THEY WANT TO SEE THE BEHIND-THE-SCENES ACTION FOR THEIR PREVIEWS--SO SHOW'EM.
GOD, RICO, I CAN'T HOLD MY BREATH FOREVER. FOR YOUR INFORMATION, THIS RUBBER STUFF ISN'T WELL VENTILATED!

ALL YOU DO IS COMPLAIN, SIMONE. NOW C'MON, LOOK KINKY.
JUST HURRY. I CAN'T KEEP THIS POSE MUCH LONGER!
IF PRESSED SHE'D ADMIT THAT WITH FOUR KIDS OF HER OWN AND NO HUSBAND, AUNT RHONDA DOESN'T HAVE MUCH TIME FOR HER, AND SARA--WELL, SARA SEEMS TO BE PREOCCUPIED AS OF LATE.
SO YEAH, MAYBE SHE DOES WANT ATTENTION
BUT NOW, SHE THINKS, IS THIS WHAT I HAD IN MIND?
ONE DAY, I'M GOING TO BE HOSTING MY OWN SHOW ON MTV AND I WON'T HAVE TO FOLLOW YOUR STUPID ORDERS!

WOW.
CAMERON, I'M STILL ON MILAN TIME. HOW LONG UNTIL OUR NEXT APPOINTMENT?
ONE HOUR AND TWENTY MINUTES.
OH MY GOD! SHE'S HERE! THEY SAID SHE DIDN'T HAVE TIME TO STOP IN. LISA, I'M NOT SUPPOSED TO HAVE YOU BACK HERE.
WHO--?
WELL, WELL. LOOKS LIKE THE FETISH BALL FASHION SHOW IN HERE. MS. BOUCHER, THESE "GIRLS" HARDLY SEEM THE TYPE--
JULIAN, THEY DON'T HAVE TO SEEM THE TYPE--THEY JUST HAVE TO LOOK THE TYPE.
THERE IS A DIFFERENCE.
WELL, NOW. THERE'S A FACE.
THIS IS IT.
UH, MS-- MS. BOUCHER, I'M LINDSEY WELLS. I'VE BEEN WITH YOUR FIRM FOR TWO YEARS NOW--
LOOK AT THIS FACE. CAMERON, TAKE A NOTE TO CALL MISS WELLS REGARDING-- WHAT IS YOUR NAME, DARLING?
L-LISA BUZANIS, MS. BOUCHER.
LISA, I ADORE YOUR LOOK. YOU HAVE THE FRESH SCRUBBED IMAGE I'M AFTER FOR OUR SPRING SHOWS.
JULIAN, CALL FOR THE LIMO. I'M FAMISHED.

L'AMAZON RESTAURANT. 2:45 P.M.
...YES, I'LL BE PLAYING A FEW ACOUSTIC SONGS, BUT YOU, MR. IRONS, YOU WILL BE THE HIGHLIGHT OF THE FUNDRAISER.
AND I MUST SAY, YOUR RESTAURANT IS **BREATHTAKING!**
REALLY, GORDON, YOU FLATTER ME SO.
PLEASE, CALL ME STING.
I DON'T GET THE CHANCE TO VISIT THE AMAZON NEARLY AS MUCH AS I USED TO, SO I BROUGHT A LITTLE OF IT BACK TO NEW YORK.
HERE, YOU CAN ENJOY ALL THE SIGHTS AND SOUNDS OF THE RAINFOREST WITHOUT GETTING **WATER-LOGGED.**
I KNOW MR. NOTTINGHAM HERE, PREFERS IT THAT WAY. EH, IAN?
UH, MR. IRONS, NOT TO CHANGE THE SUBJECT, BUT ABOUT YOUR CONTRIBUTION. I'LL JUST NEED A BALL PARK NUMBER FOR THE NEWS REPORTERS AND PRESS RELEASES.
OH, OF COURSE.

NOTTINGHAM, WHAT DID I QUOTE THIS MORNING?
YOU DAMNED BASTARD!
PERHAPS YOU'D LIKE TO KEEP YOUR RUDE COMMENTS TO YOURSELF AND ANSWER THE QUESTION?
PERHAPS NOT, KEN.
I DARESAY, I BELIEVE YOU WERE EAVESDROPPING ON MY CONVERSATION WHILE TIED UP IN MY OFFICE, HEH--
IAN, YOU'RE DELIRIOUS FROM THIS MORNING. IS THIS HOW YOU THANK ME? HOW EASILY YOU FORGET WHO SAVED YOUR LIFE, WHO BROUGHT YOU BACK TO CONSCIOUSNESS.
I DIDN'T ASK TO BE.
ER, UM, I-- WELL--YOU KNOW, I REALLY DON'T NEED TO KNOW RIGHT NOW--
AH! MY APOLOGIES TO YOU AND MR. NOTTINGHAM. I'VE BEEN VERY BUSY AND--

--MY STAFF'S BEEN THROUGH A DOWNSIZING.
REALLY, THERE IS NO NEED FOR YOU TO APOLOGIZE, MR. IRONS.
AND I BELIEVE THE CONTRIBUTION YOU QUOTED WAS AN EVEN TWO MILLION DOLLARS--
--FOR THE FIGHT AGAINST WRONGFULLY MISTREATED CITIZENS, IN THIRD WORLD COUNTRIES.
*COUGH* TWO...? VERY WELL, TWO MILLION, IT IS!
YOU ARE TOO GENEROUS, MR. IRONS.
BUT FOR THAT, I'LL EXPECT YOU TO TAKE REQUESTS DURING YOUR SHOW!
I'M KIDDING, OF COURSE.
HAHAHAH!

4:10 P.M.
SAME BUILDING.
IRON'S INTERNATIONAL INVESTMENT & HOLDINGS. I SEE.
YOU CERTAINLY ARE AN INTERESTING MAN, KEN.
SO IT WAS YOU WHO SENT ME THE FLOWERS,
IRON'S INTERNATIONAL INVESTMENT & HOLDINGS, PLEASE HOLD.
IRON'S INTER-- DAVEN! HOLD A SEC, I'VE GOT TWO CONFERENCE CALLS TO PATCH INTO MR. IRONS.
NO, I TOLD YOU I'M WORKING THROUGH LUNCH. HE'S HAVING THIS HUGE MEETING--A VERY LARGE DEAL. OKAY. BYE.
IRONS
WELL, THIS CERTAINLY ISN'T WHERE THE OFFICE ACTION IS.
AH, HERE WE GO.
MR. NOTTINGHAM, MR. IRONS TOLD ME YOU HAVE SOME OF THE RAREST JAPANESE SWORDS ON THIS EARTH. HE SAID YOU MIGHT SHOW ME--
--OH, HE DID, DID HE?
EXIT
THERE REALLY IS NO SUCH THING AS A "SECURED" FLOOR.
REGULATION FIRE EXITS ARE SUPPOSED TO HAVE "STOREROOM" LOCKS INSTALLED SO THAT YOU CAN ONLY GO THROUGH A DOOR ONE WAY, AND NOT REENTER--

--BUT MORE OFTEN THAN NOT, CONTRACTORS JUST PUT IN UNLOCKABLE DOORS TO ALLEVIATE LAWSUITS IF A LOCK SHOULD JAM DURING A FIRE.
SUITS ME JUST FINE.
THIS IS A NICE OFFICE, KEN.
I'LL BET SOME HIGH-POWERED MEETINGS GO ON IN THESE CONF--
--30 BILLION IS MY OFFER.
I'M AFRAID WE DON'T HAVE MORE LIQUID CAPITAL.
COME, MR. AFZALI, FOR 10 MORE, I'M SURE WE COULD FIND A VERY--
--SMOOTH TRANSITION IN SELLING THAT OIL...
...UH, GENTLEMEN, EXCUSE ME FOR A MOMENT.
OHMIGOD, HOW DID HE KNOW?
EXIT
MS. PEZZINI, YOU SEEM TO HAVE SOME INTEREST IN ME AFTER ALL.
PITY YOU HAD TO FLEE. NO MATTER, WE'LL MEET AGAIN.
MY APOLOGIES, GENTLEMEN. NOW, WHERE WERE WE?

11:55 P.M.
THE IDEA THAT ASSAULT OR HOMICIDE CANNOT BE COMMITTED IN PUBLIC SPACES IS A FALLACY. MURDERERS KNOW NO BOUNDARIES.
HAHAH-YESSSS.
FROM THE INSIDE OF EXECUTIVE BOARD ROOMS, TO THE DARK ALLEYS, OR ON A SUBWAY PLATFORM --IN NEW YORK, NO ONE IS SAFE.
ESPECIALLY NOT A YOUNG MODEL VENTURING FAR AWAY FROM HOME. YES, THE CITY'S A VERY SCARY PLACE.
HUFF HUFF PLEASE-- LEAVE ME ALONE!
AND IT'S NOT JUST THE CRIMINALS THAT ARE FRIGHTENING--IT'S THE BYSTANDER'S INDIFFERENCE.
THEY'VE GOT THEIR KIDS TO GO HOME TO. NO TIME TO GET INVOLVED WITH A MURDER. PAPERWORK ALONE WOULD TAKE YOU TWO HOURS.
AGGHH-- SOMEBODY HELLPP-- MMEEE!
VGGZZZTT!
BUT MOST OF ALL, AS LONG AS IT'S NOT A FRIEND OR A RELATIVE, NO ONE REALLY CARES.
AND THIS GIRL, THE THIRD WITHIN DAYS TO BE EXECUTED BY THE INFAMOUS "MICROWAVE" MURDERER, WAS NO FRIEND OR RELATIVE OF THESE BYSTANDERS.
NOR WERE THEY INTERESTED IN RECEIVING THE SAME FATE, AS THEY CASUALLY TURNED THEIR HEADS AND WATCHED THE CLOAKED FIGURE DEPART AS THEIR TRAIN APPROACHED.
THEY LEFT A BURNT HUSK OF A WOMAN BEHIND AND TRIED TO QUICKLY DELETE WHAT THEY'D SEEN FROM THEIR MINDS AS THEY RODE HOME.

3:25 A.M.
THE P.I.'S RESOURCE DEPARTMENT'S A PRETTY DEAD PLACE THESE DAYS. IT'S EASIER TO HAND SOME BUM A FIVE DOLLAR BILL THAN TO BANG ON A COMPUTER.
MOST OF THE INFO IN THESE COMPUTERS AREN'T WORTH A DAMN WHEN DEALING WITH 16 YEAR OLD MURDERERS.
BUT, THEY ARE GOOD FOR FINDING INFORMATION ABOUT A PERSON WHO IS PROMINENT ENOUGH TO HAVE A PUBLIC FILE.
HEY, COOPER. OH, NOTHING MUCH. JUST WORKING. OH, I HAVE SOMETHING YOU'D BE INTERESTED IN--MY SISTER JUST LEFT ME A MESSAGE TELLING ME SHE'S FLYING IN FOR A LITTLE STAY. YOU AND HER HIT IT OFF LAST TIME, DIDN'T YOU?
YOU KNOW, COOP, I CAN'T BE HELD RESPONSBLE FOR HER. JUST BECAUSE SHE LEFT YOU STRANDED IN BROOKLYN WITH YOUR PANTS DOWN, DOESN'T MEAN IT'S MY FAULT. HAHA.
BUT, BACK TO BUSINESS. WHAT'D YOU FIND? NOTHING? ARE YOU SURE? WHAT ABOUT LISTED UNDER JUST IRONS INTERNATIONAL? YOU'RE KIDDING! HE'S SQUEAKY CLEAN?
LOOK, DON'T GO OFF ON ME. I NEVER REALLY PAID ATTENTION TO HIM. YOU KNOW I DON'T WATCH TV.
THE NEWS? COOP, MY JOB DOESN'T AFFORD ME THE LUXURY TO HEAR WATERED-DOWN, SENSATIONALISTIC CRAP. YEAH, YEAH. BYE.
KENNETH IRONS. YOU REALLY WANT TO BUY ME COFFEE?
GOD, IT'S BEEN A LONG DAY...

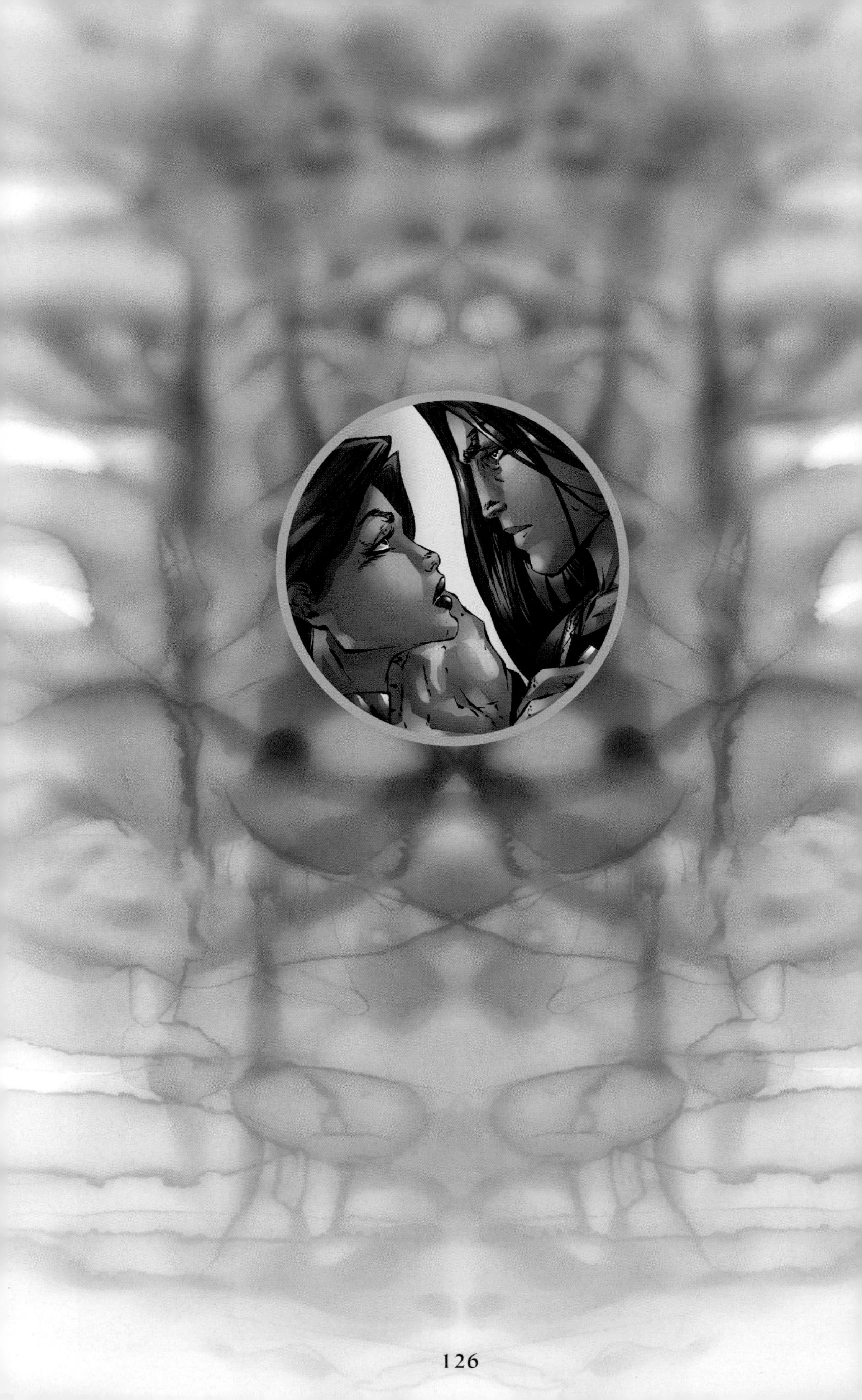

I SEE I'M NOT ALONE ANYMORE.
IT-- IT'S GONE.
I NEED YOU, SARA--
YOU MAY FEEL RELEASED, BUT THE WITCHBLADE STILL SURROUNDS YOU. THAT I KNOW.
THESE DOORS ARE NOT OPEN TO ME.
BUT YOU HAVE ACCESS. I CAN HELP YOU UNDERSTAND, IF YOU PAY MY PRICE.
HERE'S A CONNECTION YOU'VE FAILED TO SEE.
AND ONE YOU JUST DON'T UNDERSTAND.
THIS-- IS PART OF ME?
EVERYTHING HERE IS A PART OF YOU.

YOU DON'T NEED TO BE AFRAID.
YOU ARE TRANSFORMED AND WILL NEVER BE THE SAME. ACCEPT IT.
YOU WANT SO BADLY TO BE A HERO, DO YOU NOT?
I CAN TAKE YOU.
SO VIOLENT.
YOU'RE POWERLESS HERE.
BUT I AM FREE HERE.

FORGIVE ME FOR NOT BEING ABLE TO COMPLETE MY ASSIGNMENT --FOR NOT BEING ABLE TO **END** YOUR LIFE AND SET YOU **COMPLETELY FREE** FROM THE CONSEQUENCES OF THE ***WITCHBLADE.***
PERHAPS THERE IS ***ANOTHER*** WAY...
...ANOTHER DOOR. LOOK!
WHAT WE'VE ***FOUND*** MUST NEVER--

--STOP!?!

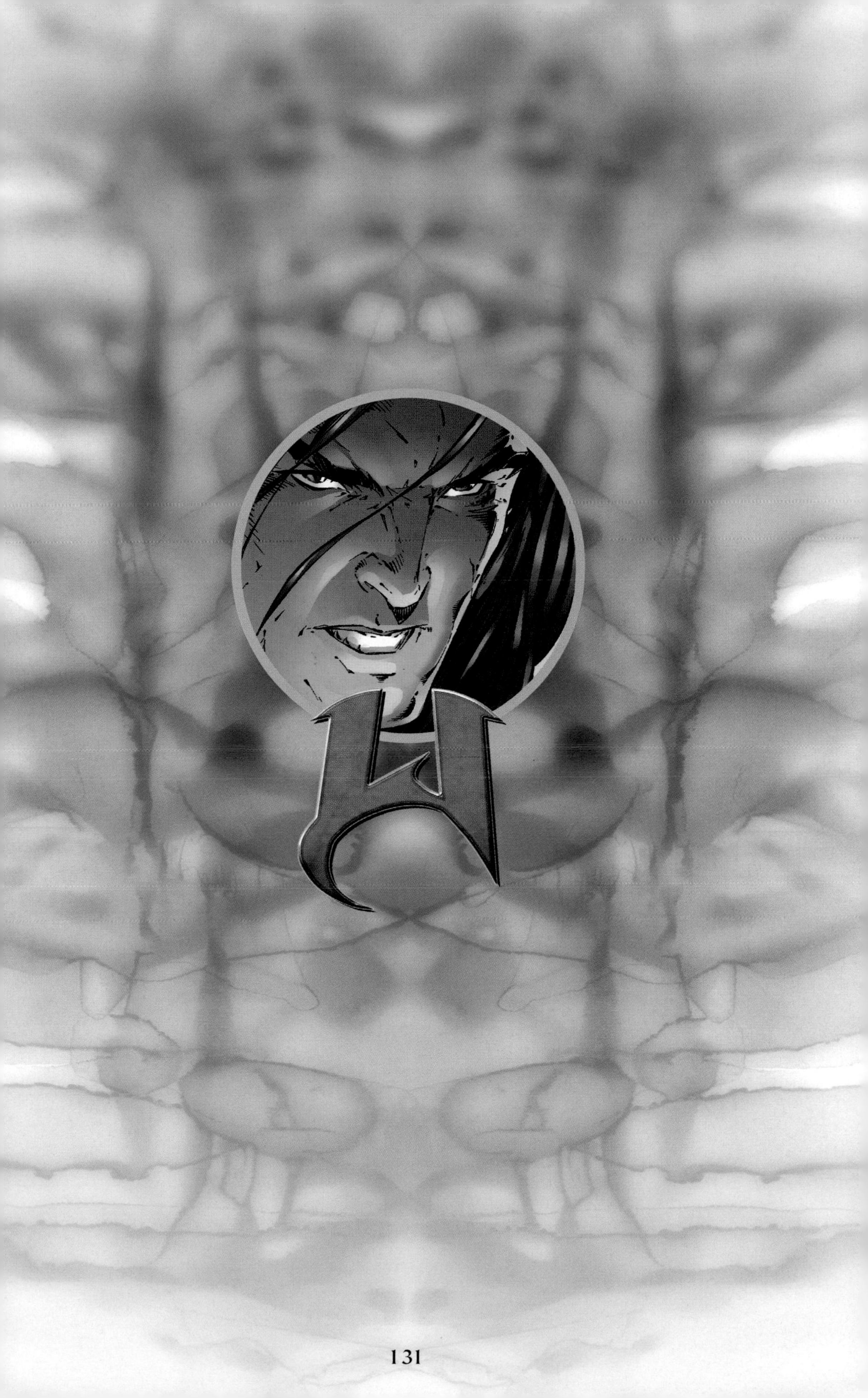

# ISSUE #6

story: **David Wohl** and **Christina Z.**
pencils and co-plot: **Michael Turner**
inks: **D-Tron**
colors: **JD Smith**

CALVARY CEMETERY, 11:30 A.M.
...AND AS WE LAY MICHAEL YEE TO REST, I AM REMINDED OF THE WRITINGS OF A.L. FRINK:
-AHEM- NEAR SHADY WALL A ROSE ONCE GREW, BUDDED AND BLOSSOMED IN GOD'S FREE LIGHT, WATERED AND FED BY MORNING DEW, SHEDDING ITS SWEETNESS DAY AND NIGHT.
AS IT GREW AND BLOSSOMED FAIR AND TALL, SLOWLY RISING TO LOFTIER HEIGHT, IT CAME UPON A CREVICE IN THE WALL THROUGH WHICH THERE SHONE A BEAM OF LIGHT.
ONWARD IT CREPT WITH ADDED STRENGTH WITH NEVER A THOUGHT OF FEAR OR PRIDE, IT FOLLOWED THE LIGHT THROUGH THE CREVICE'S LENGTH AND UNFOLDED ITSELF ON THE OTHER SIDE.
...SHALL CLAIM OF DEATH CAUSE US TO GRIEVE AND MAKE OUR COURAGE FAINT OR FALL? NO! LET US FAITH AND HOPE RECEIVE-- THE ROSE STILL GROWS BEYOND THE WALL,
SCATTERING FRAGRANCE FAR AND WIDE JUST AS IT DID IN DAYS OF YORE, JUST AS IT DID ON THE OTHER SIDE, JUST AS IT WILL FOREVER-MORE.
WHY COULDN'T IT HAVE BEEN RAINING?

IT'S SUCH A BEAUTIFUL DAY. LIKE YOU'RE NOT EVEN DEAD.
MOST OF THESE GUYS--AS SOON AS THEY GET OUT OF HERE, THEY'RE GONNA FIRE UP THE BARBECUE, TAKE THE KIDS TO THE PARK.
LIKE YOU'RE NOT EVEN GONE.
MICHAEL. I DON'T WANT TO LET YOU GO. MAYBE I **SHOULD** HAVE SEEN THE GRIEVANCE COUNSELOR. MAYBE I JUST REALLY NEEDED TO TAKE SOME TIME AND MOURN LIKE **REAL** PEOPLE DO.
HARD TO NOT BE PREOCCUPIED WITH THE OTHER STUFF THAT'S BEEN GOING ON: THE DREAM, KEN IRONS, THIS...**THING** ON MY WRIST.
THE DREAM...HE CALLED IT...THE **WITCHBLADE.**
AND WHILE I'M HEADING MY OWN PERSONAL INVESTIGATION, THE MAN WHO ORDERED YOUR DEATH IS STILL OUT THERE. I KNOW, BECAUSE HE NEARLY **KILLED** ME!
SO, HERE I AM, BLINKING BACK TEARS SO NO ONE WILL SEE ME CRY. AND IF I DID, WOULD THESE TEARS BE ONLY FOR YOU, MICHAEL? WOULD THEY BE BECAUSE I KNOW YOU'LL NEVER SEE YOUR DAUGHTER GROW UP?
OR DO YOU SUPPOSE IT WOULD BE FOR EVERYTHING THAT'S HAPPENED TO ME THESE PAST FEW DAYS.
AND HERE, YOUR FAMILY MOURNS YOU PROPERLY. WITH TEARS AND SOBS. WHY AM I SO CONCERNED WITH BEING COMPOSED AND NOBLE ABOUT THIS?
PART OF ME WANTS TO BREAK DOWN AND THE OTHER PART WANTS TO BE LIKE STEEL--SO THAT **NOTHING** CAN GET TO ME.

BUT MICHAEL, I'M STAYING STRONG FOR YOU. YOU WOULD'VE WANTED IT THAT WAY. TO ACT-- LIKE YOU'RE NOT EVEN DEAD.
GOD KNOWS I'LL HAVE TO.
SELZER. FOR CHRISSAKES, WHAT'S IT GONNA BE THIS TIME.
WELL, DE-TECTIVE PEZZINI.
YOU'RE LOOKING IN FINE HEALTH. YOU MUST TELL ME YOUR REJUVENATION SECRETS! MAYBE YOU SHOULD'VE TRIED SOME OUT ON YOUR PARTNER.
SELZER, GET OUTTA MY FACE--
--SHE'S STILL OFFICIALLY ON LEAVE, SELZER. STOW THE QUESTIONS A WHILE.
JOE SIRY. ALWAYS THERE FOR ME.
HOW YA DOING, KIDDO?
SARA, I'M ALWAYS AVAILABLE IF YOU WANT TO TALK ABOUT ANYTHING. YOU KNOW MY NUMBER. DALIA MISSES YOUR LATE-NIGHT CALLS, ANYWAY.
PEZ!
THANKS, CHIEF.
NICE OUTFIT, HUH.
NOT QUITE AS HOT AS WHAT SHE WORE TO THE RIALTO, BUT STILL NICE.
WHATEVER.
I'M GONNA WALK FOR A WHILE, JOE. MAYBE CATCH A CAB. THAT LIMO'S KINDA DEPRESSING.
SURE... TAKE IT EASY.

PEZ! SARA! WHERE'RE YOU--?!?
AHH. DON'T EVEN WAIT 'TIL YEE'S BODY COOLS, EH, JAKE? NOW THAT'S A DESPERATE MAN.
STILL, I WOULDN'T MESS WITH HER IF I WERE YOU. SHE'S ONE OF THOSE PSYCHO-BITCHES.
GREAT BOD, THOUGH. MIGHT BE WORTH IT.
YOU HEAR HER STORY ABOUT THE RIALTO? SOUNDED PRETTY SHADY TO ME. I'LL BET YEE TRIED TO GET A PIECE OF HER ACTION. MAYBE SHE LIKED IT. MAYBE THINGS GOT OUTTA HANDDDGGGLLL
GNNGH-- C-COME ON! DO IT! HIT ME--YOU SORRY-ASSED, WIMPY BASTARD!
I--I-- I'M GONNA--
G--GONNA WHAT? HUH? I'LL ~KOFF~ HAVE YOUR BADGE SO FAST--
YOU KNOW WHAT? YOU'RE NOT WORTH MY TIME.
"I'VE GOT MORE IMPORTANT THINGS TO TAKE CARE OF."

WHERE AM I GOING?
FOR SOME REASON, I THOUGHT WALKING A FEW BLOCKS WOULD MIRACULOUSLY PUT MY LIFE IN ORDER.
SURPRISE. IT DIDN'T.
GOT TO RETRACE MY STEPS, RETHINK MY SITUATION. START ACTING LIKE A COP AGAIN. SOMETHING I HAVEN'T DONE FOR A WHILE.
Au Bon Pain
COFFEE ESPRESSO BAKERY
FUNNY, BACK WHEN I WAS IN THE ACADEMY, A PSYCHOLOGIST THERE TOLD ME I WAS ONE OF THE MORE "TOGETHER" PEOPLE HE'D INTERVIEWED. HE ASKED IF I REALLY WANTED TO GET INTO HOMICIDE.
HE FIGURED I'D GET DESENSITIZED LIKE MOST OF THE DETECTIVES AROUND HERE. SOME OF THOSE GUYS COULD MAKE A JOKE WHEN THEY SEE A YOUNG BOY BLOW A HOLE IN HIS MOTHER FOR FOOD STAMPS. IT'S NOT SUPPOSED TO GET ME DOWN. BUT IT DOES.
AU BON PAIN
HOW PEOPLE HAVE SUCH DISREGARD FOR HUMAN LIFE WILL FOREVER BE A MYSTERY TO ME. AND THOSE ARE THE GOOD GUYS.
AND MY DREAM. WHAT DID IT MEAN? THE MAN WITH THE SWORD. THOSE VERY HANDS THAT IN REALITY, HURT ME--WERE IN MY DREAM STATE, CARESSING ME.

OH DAMN. IT'S THE 10TH AND I STILL HAVEN'T PAID MY RENT. DAMMIT.
SIGH...

HOW 'BOUT THAT COFFEE, SARA?
I KNOW THAT VOICE.

I KNOW WHO I'M GOING TO SEE WHEN I LOOK UP.
IT'S HIM.

I SAW YOU WALKING OUT OF THE CEMETERY. I'M SORRY ABOUT YOUR PARTNER--MICHAEL, WAS IT? I READ ABOUT IT IN THE PAPER.
I JUST WANTED TO EXPRESS MY SYMPATHY BUT WHEN I SAW YOU AT THE GYM--
--KEN, WHY ARE YOU FOLLOWING ME?
FOLLOWING?
HMM, I RECALL ONE PARTICULAR LADY DOING SOME RATHER GOOD INVESTIGATIVE WORK AT MY OFFICE...
AH, WELL--YOU DID GIVE ME YOUR CARD.
I SENT YOU THOSE FLOWERS IN THE HOSPITAL BECAUSE--I HAD A SIMILAR EXPERIENCE AND I REMEMBER WHAT IT FELT LIKE.
I WANTED TO TALK TO YOU ABOUT WHAT HAPPENED ON LIBERTY ISLAND.
YES, THAT. HOW HAS THE WITCHBLADE BEEN TREATING YOU?
THE--YOU--KNOW--NO. NO.
STOP. WHY--OH GOD, YOU KNOW?!? WHAT THE HELL--
--SARA, WAIT. I HAVE ANSWERS FOR YOU. PLEASE. WHAT YOU HAVE IS DANGEROUS.
IF YOU COME WITH ME, I CAN HELP YOU REALIZE JUST WHAT IT IS YOU'VE... GOT ON YOU.
SARA, THANK YOU FOR THIS OPPORTUNITY. WE CAN TAKE MY CAR.
NO--I'LL GET A CAB. I'VE HAD PRETTY BAD LUCK WITH LIMOS.
KENNETH IRONS? SARA, WHAT ARE YOU GETTING YOURSELF INTO?

1:15 P.M.
A MODEL! ME! JUST LIKE CHRISTY, NAOMI, ELLE, UMA AND KATE. EEEEEE! SARA, YOU BETTER BE HOME!
C'MON. LITTLE BIT HARDER. OOOOH, YEAH. PUSH. BE GENTLE, C'MON.
CLOSER, CLOSER-- AH!
UH, HI, WHAT ARE YOU DOING? THIS IS SARA'S APARTMENT.
GOT IT! HUH? OH...
HI! YOU'RE FRIENDS WITH MY SISTER? I'M JULIE PEZZINI.
I'M FROM HOLLYWOOD. YOU KNOW I JUST FLEW INTO TOWN, AND I MUST'VE LOST MY KEY OR SOMETHING. I'VE BEEN MEETING UP WITH OLIVER STONE, HAVING AUDITIONS AND MODELING.
I JUST DID AN INCREDIBLE FASHION SHOW IN ROME. I GOT TO WEAR THE COOLEST ANNA SUI DRESS!
HEY, DON'T JUST STAND THERE. YOU CAN COME IN. SARA WON'T MIND. HOW DO YOU KNOW MY SISTER?
M...M... MODELING?

OH, DEAR SISTER, LOOK HOW NEAT YOU ARE! IF MOM COULD SEE IT NOW.
YOU KNOW, I'M JUST IN THE CITY FOR A COUPLE OF DAYS. I'VE GOT CONTACTS TO MAKE. "OUCH" MAGAZINE NEEDS A MODEL WITH A 19 INCH WAIST AND A BEAUTIFUL BACK FOR A COVER SHOT.
I INTEND TO GET THE JOB!
LET'S SEE. AH-HA! JUST WHAT THE DOCTOR ORDERED. EEW. DOUG, I SWEAR, THIS GUY NEVER GIVES UP!
HEY, HAVE A DRINK WITH ME.
Happy Birthday Pez - Love DOUG
I-- CAN'T.
UMM-- WHY??
WELL... OH, OK.
I--I'M GOING TO BE MODELING FOR BOUCHER!
BOUCHER? YOU? REALLY? WELL, DANNETTE IS INTO A CERTAIN TYPE OF FACE AND YEP, YOU'VE GOT IT! WHAT ARE YOU, TWELVE!
NOW C'MON, HURRY. I DID A SHOW FOR DANNETTE A YEAR AGO. LET'S GO PAY HER OFFICES A VISIT. MAYBE I CAN HELP YOUR CAREER. I AM IN THE KNOW!
YOU'D HELP ME? REALLY?
HEY, STICK WITH ME, AND ALL YOUR WORRIES ARE GONE. I KNOW EVERYONE! NOW, A TOAST!
TO WILD ABANDON AND DUMB MEN WITH MONEY! HAHAH! DRINK UP!

CENTRAL PARK WEST. 2:20 P.M.
GOOD AFTERNOON, SIR.
JEROME'S MY DOORMAN. ANYTIME YOU WANT TO LEAVE, JUST SAY THE WORD.
IT'S HAPPENING.
IT'S SO EXHILARATING, WISHING HE COULD TELL HER THE PLAN. JUST A LITTLE HINT. BUT NO-- IT'S NOT TIME YET.
EVEN THOUGH HE'S GONE OVER THIS IN HIS MIND THOUSANDS OF TIMES, HE STILL CAN'T BELIEVE IT'S REALLY HAPPENING.
HMM. WHERE TO BEGIN...ALL RIGHT...LONG BEFORE I BECAME A BUSINESSMAN, I WORKED WITH MY FATHER, A RENOWNED ARCHEOLOGIST, IN EGYPT. TOGETHER WE WENT ON EXPEDITION AFTER EXPEDITION.
AS A PROFESSOR AT THE UNIVERSITY OF CAIRO HE UNCOVERED MANY RARE ARTIFACTS AND A NUMBER OF MYSTERIES THAT MANKIND STILL REJECTS.
IT WAS THERE THAT WE FIRST LEARNED OF THE WITCHBLADE. THE NAME COMES FROM SEVERAL TRANSLATIONS AND HAS VERY LITTLE TO DO WITH WITCHCRAFT OR ANY-THING OF THAT SORT.
AND, AS YOU WILL SEE, IT IS MOST LIKELY CONNECTED TO A NUMBER OF HISTORIC EVENTS WHERE THE SUPERNATURAL OCCURED.
I LIKE TO THINK OF MYSELF AS WELL EDUCATED, KEN. BUT I HAVE NEVER HEARD OF ANYTHING LIKE THIS. HOW DO YOU KNOW--
I DON'T. NOT EXACTLY. BUT I HAVE COLLECTED MANY ARTIFACTS AND DOCUMENTS THAT SUGGEST WE WERE RIGHT. COME, LET ME SHOW YOU THE SMALL EXHIBIT I KEEP HERE AT MY HOUSE. PERHAPS YOU MIGHT SEE SOME SIMILARITIES.
THE HELL WITH EXPLANATIONS, HE THINKS. THE WITCHBLADE IS SO CLOSE TO BEING HIS. WHY NOT JUST DO IT?
NO. SAVOR THE MOMENT. THEY'LL SHARE A LIFETIME TOGETHER. HE AND THE WITCHBLADE.
MY FATHER AND HIS CLOSEST ASSOCIATES BELIEVED THE WITCHBLADE TO BE AN ITEM THAT IS NOT OF SOME MAGICAL MAKE UP, BUT RATHER, AN EXTRATERRESTRIAL ITEM.
IN THE SIMPLEST TERMS, WE DON'T KNOW WHERE IT COMES FROM. BUT AFTER MY FATHER DIED IN A CAVE ACCIDENT, I TOOK OVER HIS SEARCH. IT IS WHAT I SPENT MUCH OF MY LIFE DOING UNTIL I FINALLY FOUND IT DURING AN EXCAVATION IN GREECE.

OH MY GOD.
JOAN OF ARC? HEARING VOICES. OH, GOD.
THIS IS ALL INCREDIBLE. BUT HOW DOES THIS TIE IN TO WHY YOU WERE AT LIBERTY ISLAND. PLEASE EXPLAIN THAT TO ME.
NO! SHE RUINED THE MOMENT! IRONS WISHES HE COULD HIT HER--FOR DESECRATING THIS ROOM WITH MEANINGLESS CHATTER. BUT STRIKING HER WOULD BE COUNTERPRODUCTIVE.
UNBELIEVABLE, HE THINKS. HERE IN THE CHAMBER DEVOTED TO THE WITCHBLADE, WALKS ITS PRESENT WIELDER. HOW DIVINELY PRECIOUS.
JOAN OF ARC. A SAINT CLAIMING TO HEAR VOICES, URGING HER TO FIGHT AGAINST SEEMINGLY INSURMOUNTABLE ODDS DURING THE HUNDRED YEARS WAR.
IT IS WRITTEN, HER SWORD SEEMINGLY CAME TO LIFE DURING HER BATTLES. AND AFTER HER CAPTURE AT COMPIEGNE, HER WEAPON DISAPPEARED FROM HER HAND.
CURIOUSLY, SHE WAS ONLY VULNERABLE WITHOUT IT. NO ONE KNOWS WHY SHE ABANDONED IT. MAYBE TRUE MARTYRDOM. WE'LL NEVER KNOW.
IRONS KNOWS THAT SARA WILL NEVER ABANDON THE WITCHBLADE. HE'LL MAKE SURE OF THAT.
-AHRM- WELL, IAN NOTTINGHAM AND MYSELF USED TO BE CO-WORKERS ON A JOURNEY THAT TOOK US TO DELHI. HE AND I BOTH WERE VERSED IN THE WITCHBLADE.
WHILE I WANTED TO FIND THE RIGHTFUL OWNER AND EDUCATE THEM, NOTTINGHAM WANTED TO USE THE POWER FOR HIS OWN SELFISH PURPOSES. HE IS RECENTLY HERE FROM THE BRITISH ISLES AND I HAVE BEEN WATCHING HIM CAREFULLY.
I KNEW OF HIS TOURNAMENT AT THE RIALTO THEATER AND I HONESTLY DIDN'T THINK HE'D TRAIL YOU SO CLOSELY AND INTEND TO DO YOU SUCH DAMAGE. I CERTAINLY COULDN'T LET YOU GET HURT, SO I INTERVENED.

THIS URN, DATED BACK TO ROUGHLY 340BC., IS BELIEVED TO REPRESENT A MYSTERIOUS ADVISOR TO ALEXANDER THE GREAT, WHO ASSISTED THE WARRIOR IN HIS CONQUEST OF THEBES.
WHAT A WASTE, HE THINKS. SHE'LL NEVER BE ABLE TO REALLY APPRECIATE THE GRANDEUR OF THE WITCHBLADE. NOBODY CAN. EXCEPT HIM.
NOW, LOOK AROUND YOU, SARA, AT THE FORMER WIELDERS OF THE WITCHBLADE.
EGYPT'S FOURTH DYNASTY ACHIEVED UNSURPASSED GREATNESS. SUPERNATURAL FEATS WERE REPORTED ON AN ALMOST DAILY BASIS AS THIS EMPIRE ROSE.
AGAIN, THE WITCHBLADE OBVIOUSLY PLAYED A ROLE.
SO THAT'S WHY YOU'VE BEEN SO INTERESTED IN ME.
SHE SEEMS SATISFIED WITH THE EXPLANATION. TIME TO GET TO THE EXCITING PART OF HIS LECTURE.
YES, I MEAN, NO. SARA, THERE IS SOMETHING ABOUT THE WITCHBLADE I HAVEN'T TOLD YOU.

IT ONLY HAS ONE OWNER OVER A GIVEN PERIOD OF TIME. ANYONE ELSE WHO TRIES TO POSSESS IT, SHALL PERISH.
SARA, WHETHER YOU LIKE IT OR NOT-- YOU ARE A CHANGED PERSON. IT'S UP TO YOU TO DECIDE WHETHER THIS IS A LIFE YOU WANT TO LEAD.
I KNOW WHAT HAPPENED AT THE RIALTO.
I CAN HELP YOU DEAL WITH IT OR HELP YOU REMOVE IT.
I WILL ABIDE BY ANY DECISION YOU CHOOSE.
YES HE WILL, AS LONG AS IT'S THE RIGHT ONE.
OH, IF ONLY THIS COARSE POLICE WOMAN COULD TRULY ENJOY WHAT IS HAPPENING.
THEY COULD LAUGH AND SHARE A COGNAC BEFORE THEY BEGAN THE PROCEDURE.
BUT NO, SHE'S NOT THE TYPE TO APPRECIATE SUCH FINERIES.
HE CAN'T TAKE MUCH MORE.
TIME TO BEGIN.
PLEASE, FEEL FREE TO LOOK AROUND. ALL OF THIS IS NOW A CONNECTION. A CONNECTION TO YOU.
HMM? WHAT A BEAUTIFUL TAPESTRY.
YES, HE SECRETLY IMPLORES HER-- GO THROUGH THE DOOR. GO ON. LET IT BEGIN RIGHT HERE. RIGHT NOW.
BUT THEN THE BUSINESSMAN IN HIM TAKES OVER. IT IS NOT THE RIGHT TIME. HE MUST BE PATIENT. HE'S WAITED OVER 80 YEARS FOR THIS MOMENT. WHAT'S ANOTHER COUPLE DAYS?
I'M SORRY, MISS PEZZINI. BUT I HAVE A MEETING I MUST ATTEND TO. I'LL SHOW YOU TO THE DOOR.

7:05 P.M. 28TH ST. IRT STATION.
ELECTRICAL'S BEEN TRIPPED SINCE THE MURDER. SUBWAY'S NOT RUNNING. NEARLY COLLIDED WITH ANOTHER TRAIN. WHY ISN'T ANYONE CONNECTING THIS?
MICROWAVE MURDERER. DAMMIT. WE SHOULD HAVE MORE LEADS THAN THIS!
NO BLOOD. NO FIBERS. NO PRINTS AND NO WITNESSES. IT'S GOT TO BE CONNECTED.
IT'S ALL CONNECTED. EVEN I KNOW THAT!
WHO?
THE MURDERS AT THE RIALTO, HONEY POT, LIBERTY ISLAND. LET ME GUESS--YOU'RE ONE OF THE "DICKS" ON THIS CASE WHO WON'T TALK TO ME, RIGHT?
I WORK FOR WGOR, CHANNEL 81. MY NAME'S BECCA. COPS HATE ME 'CAUSE I FIND STUFF OUT THEY CAN'T. I'M A BETTER INVESTIGATOR AND I'LL PUT MY LIFE ON THE LINE FOR IT.
GROAN WHAT IS YOUR POINT IN ALL THIS.
MY POINT IS-- YOU'RE THE FIRST COP I'VE SEEN WHO'S PAID ANY ATTENTION TO THESE MURDERS.
THE RIALTO FIASCO? ALL THOSE CONS DIE AND NO ONE DOES A THING ABOUT IT? I MEAN, I KNOW THEY'RE CROOKS AND ALL, BUT THEY GOT FAMILIES, TOO. NOT A PEEP FROM THE COPS.
FRIEND OF MINE TOOK A LOOK AND SAID POLICE TAPE HASN'T EVEN BEEN BROKEN THERE YET! BY THE WAY, WHAT'S YOUR NAME?
I'M JAKE. AND YES, I AM INVESTIGATING. PLEASE CONTINUE.
WELL, SEEMS THIS SCARY GUY'D BEEN LOOMING AROUND THE PLACE BEFORE IT HAPPENED. I MEAN, THAT PLACE WASN'T EVEN OPEN FOR BUSINESS. IT HAD TO GET ALL REMODELED SOMEHOW. AND YOU AND I BOTH KNOW THOSE KINDA PERMITS AREN'T EASY TO GET-- GOTTA PAY TAX ON IT AND EVERYTHING.
SOO--WHAT I'M SAYIN', IS THAT HOW COME NOTHING'S BEEN DONE BY THE COPS? I'LL TELL YOU HOW COME! BECAUSE THEY'RE TOO FREAKED BY THIS GUY--THEY CALL HIM MR. NOTTINGHAM. THE RUMORS WITH THE HOMELESS AROUND IS THAT HE PAID THEM OFF TO TURN THEIR BACKS. YOU HEAR ME? PAID THEM OFF.
TELL ME MORE...

7:40 P.M.
SARA, I KNOW THIS IS A LOT FOR YOU TO ABSORB, BUT THERE'S SO MUCH YOU STILL NEED TO KNOW.
I WANT TO SEE YOU TOMORROW AND TELL YOU MORE.
I KNOW. THERE IS SO MUCH. BUT I HAVE TO SAY THAT IT'S BEGINNING TO MAKE SOME SENSE...
...THE PEOPLE COMING AFTER ME... THAT ONE YOU KNOW... IAN NOTTINGHAM... I'LL DEFINITELY CALL YOU.
HE SHOULD BE OF NO CONCERN TO YOU RIGHT NOW. HERE--LET ME HAIL YOU A CAB.
NO THANKS. IT'S SUCH A BEAUTIFUL NIGHT. I'LL JUST WALK THROUGH THE PARK.
ALL RIGHT. I TRUST YOU KNOW HOW TO TAKE CARE OF YOURSELF, DETECTIVE.
SARA, THINGS WILL GET BETTER.
I KNOW THEY WILL, KEN.
YES, I THINK I CAN TAKE CARE OF MYSELF HERE.
I LOVE THIS TIME OF NIGHT HERE. CENTRAL PARK--THE PRETTIEST PLACE IN MANHATTAN WITHOUT A COVER CHARGE.
UNFORTUNATELY, IT'S ALSO ONE OF THE MOST DANGEROUS AFTER DARK. HOW IRONIC. I'VE NEVER HAD A PROBLEM HERE, THOUGH--EVEN BEFORE I WAS ISSUED MY .357.
CHK! CHK!
--MOVEMENT. FROM OVER THERE.
CHILL OUT, I'M GETTING PARANOID. PROBABLY A SQUIRREL.
SSSSK!
NO, THAT'S SOMEONE.
KLIK!

OKAY. RELAX. SCAN.
SCAN. OKAY. NOTHING.
OKAY--
IT'S HIM. IT'S IAN--
NOTTINGHAM.
GASP
FREEZE!
I SAID
FREEZE!
BLAM!
BLAM!
BLAM!
HE MAY'VE BEEN
ABLE TO TAKE ON
THE WITCHBLADE.
BUT THIS TIME
I'M BETTER PREPAID.
THESE BULLETS
HAVE TAKEN DOWN
MEN BIGGER
THAN HIM.

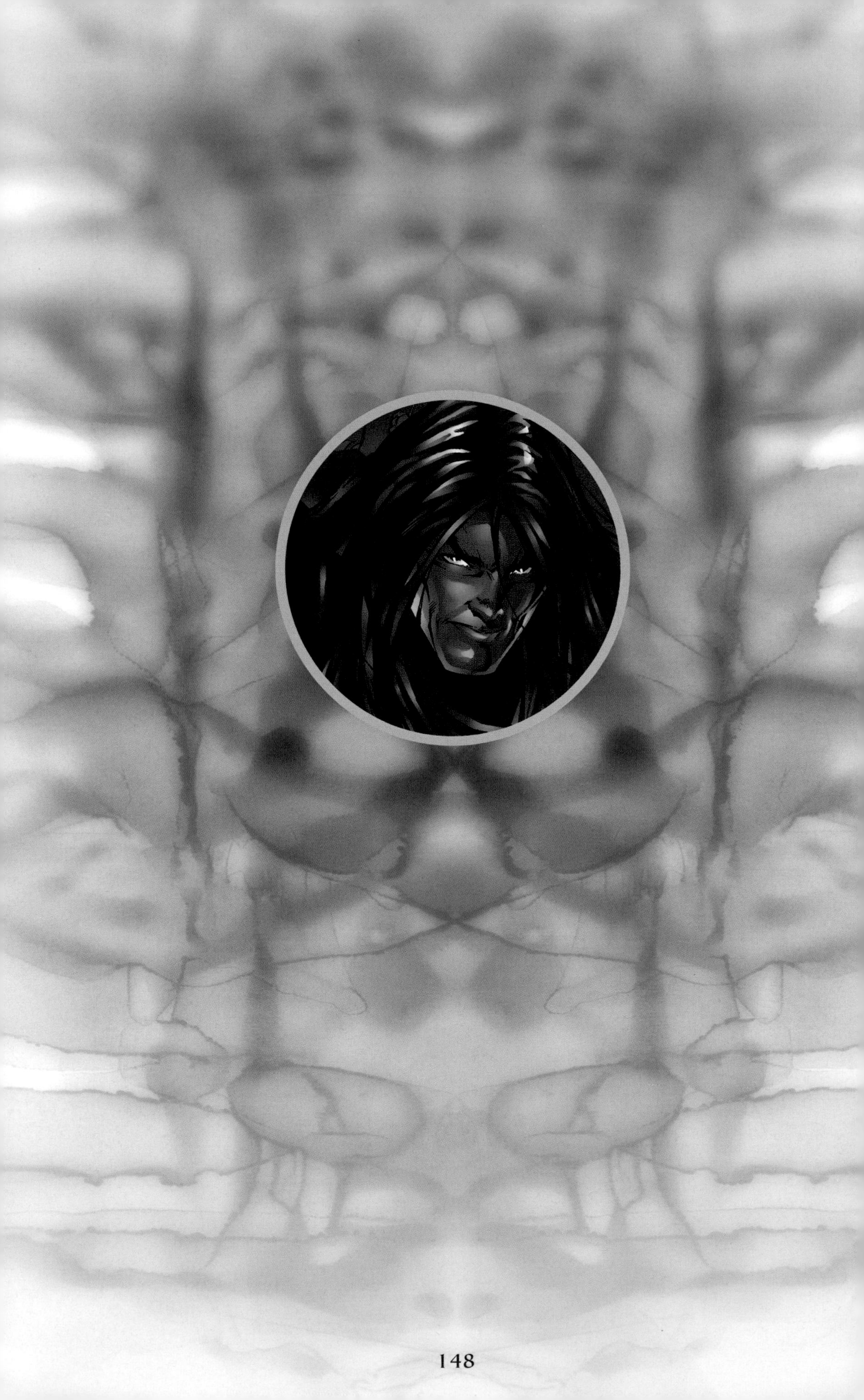

I--I UNLOADED INTO HIM--
OOOLPH!
NNNN-- DON'T FIGHT --ME!
TOO BAD PERPS DON'T REALLY FALL DOWN RIGHT WHEN THEY GET SHOT. THAT ONLY HAPPENS IN THE MOVIES--WAIT--
KRAWWWWW
OKAY. ASSESS THE SITUATION. I KNOW AT LEAST TWO BULLETS MUST'VE PENETRATED HIS CHEST CAVITY. JUST HAVE TO WAIT HIM OUT.
--NO. HE'S CLOSE-- I HAVE TO FIND A WAY OUT.
SSSSK!
PANT PANT
OH, I NEED YOU NOW. W--WITCHBLADE, PLEASE WORK. PLEASE. WHY WON'T YOU DO SOMETHING? ANYTHING?
WORK!
GOD-- PLEASE!
THIS CAN'T BE...

A DIRTY FIGHTER. I LIKE THAT.
BUT IF YOU RUN, YOU LEAVE ME NO CHOICE.

WWHOOOSH!
UNHH...
UUGGH-- UULLL-- PANT PANT

AAAGH!
NNGGG--UNH
PANT
PANT

MS. PEZZINI... I JUST WANT TO *TALK!*

## issue #7

story: **David Wohl** and **Christina Z.**
pencils and co-plot: **Michael Turner**
inks: **D-Tron**
colors: **JD Smith**

THE HAMPTONS. 7:45 P.M.
JULIE, YOU SAID IT WAS A GIFT. I DIDN'T KNOW I HAD TO SHARE.
BUT YOU DID ALL OF IT??
MM-HM.
WELL JULIE, IT SURE IS A SMALL WORLD. CAN'T BELIEVE YOU KNOW THIS LITTLE COMMODITY. SHE WAS JUST INTERVIEWING IN MY OFFICE THIS AFTERNOON.
YEAH, SHE LIVES IN MY SISTER'S APARTMENT BUILDING. SHE SORT OF SNEAKED UP ON ME. OH AND HEY, I HOPE YOU DON'T THINK SHE'LL BE YOUR ONLY COMMODITY. I DID GET THE COVER OF "OUCH!" MAGAZINE!
SWEET PEA, YOU PLAY IT RIGHT, YOU'LL GO FAR, BUT I AM GLAD YOU BROUGHT HER ALONG. SHE CAN BE... CHUCKLE ...INITIATED.
UM, WHY'D YOU LEAVE YOUR ASSISTANT CAMERON IN THE TRUNK OF THE LIMO?
MMM...SOME PEOPLE, LISA, ARE INTO UNCONVENTIONAL MEANS OF FUN.
MS. BOUCHER, PLEASE COME IN. THIS GATHERING WOULDN'T BE COMPLETE WITHOUT YOU.
OB-VIOUSLY!
CHILDREN-- STAY CLOSE. THERE'S MUCH TO SEE.
I'M--IN HEAVEN!!
IN A WAY --YES.

THERE, THERE, DID THAT **HURT?**
YOU WANTED TO **SEE** WHAT IT WAS LIKE TO BE BLINDFOLDED, SO NOW STOP SQUIRMING AND **THINK** ABOUT WHERE MY NEXT LASH WILL STRIKE YOU.

MISS BOUCHER! I'VE BEEN WAITING.
WHO DID YOU END UP BRINGING WITH YOU?
AREN'T THEY WONDERFUL, RACHEL? THEY'LL BE HERE FOR A FEW DAYS. YOU DID MAKE ALL THE PREPARATIONS I ASKED OF YOU?
OH, YES.
WOW-- THESE PEOPLE ARE FOR REAL!
UM--WHY IS SHE GOING TO HURT THAT MAN?
CHILL-- YOU'VE GOT A COUPLE DAYS TO LEARN ABOUT WHY.

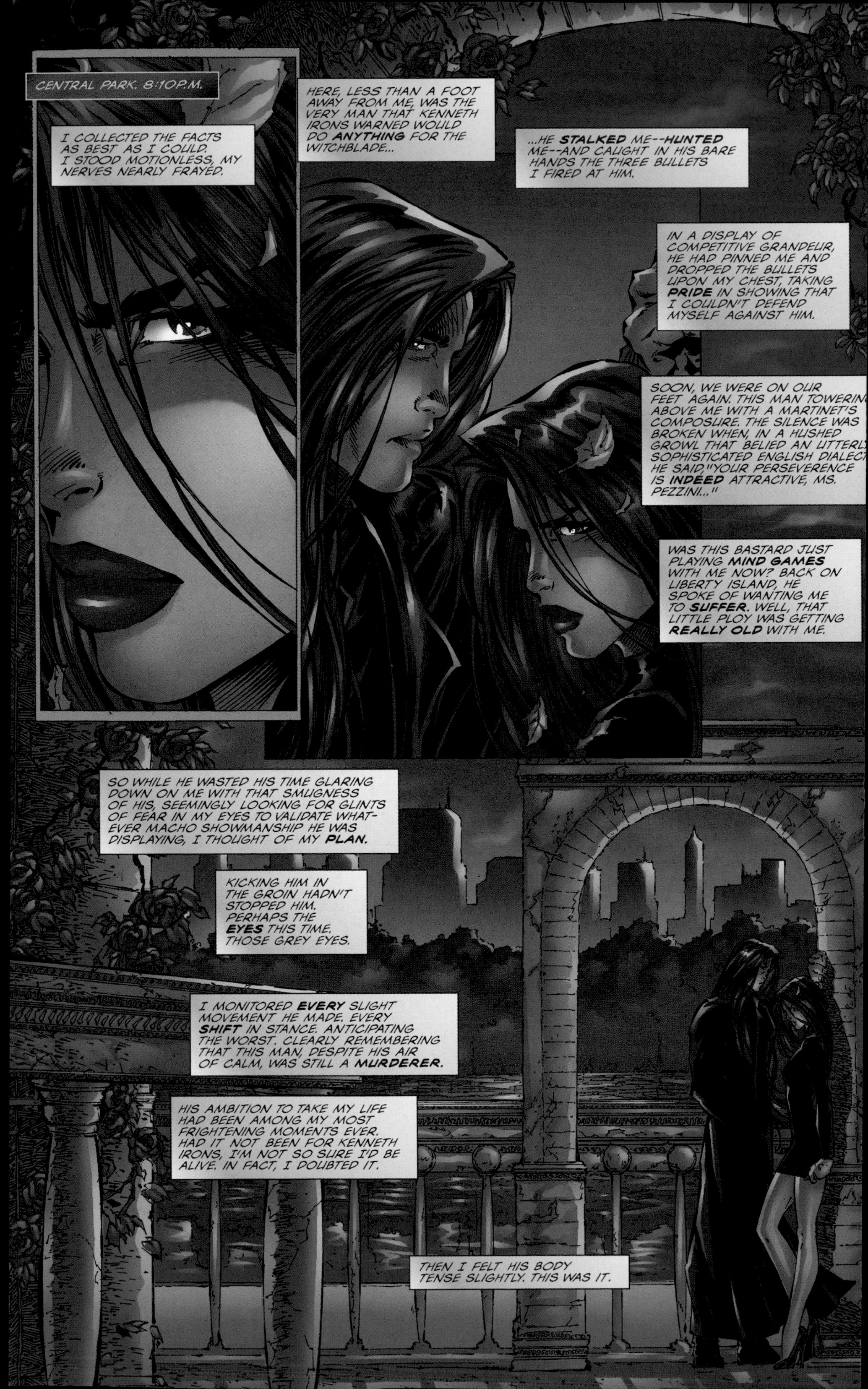
CENTRAL PARK. 8:10P.M.
I COLLECTED THE FACTS AS BEST AS I COULD. I STOOD MOTIONLESS, MY NERVES NEARLY FRAYED.
HERE, LESS THAN A FOOT AWAY FROM ME, WAS THE VERY MAN THAT KENNETH IRONS WARNED WOULD DO ANYTHING FOR THE WITCHBLADE...
...HE STALKED ME--HUNTED ME--AND CAUGHT IN HIS BARE HANDS THE THREE BULLETS I FIRED AT HIM.
IN A DISPLAY OF COMPETITIVE GRANDEUR, HE HAD PINNED ME AND DROPPED THE BULLETS UPON MY CHEST, TAKING PRIDE IN SHOWING THAT I COULDN'T DEFEND MYSELF AGAINST HIM.
SOON, WE WERE ON OUR FEET AGAIN. THIS MAN TOWERING ABOVE ME WITH A MARTINET'S COMPOSURE. THE SILENCE WAS BROKEN WHEN, IN A HUSHED GROWL THAT BELIED AN UTTERLY SOPHISTICATED ENGLISH DIALECT HE SAID,"YOUR PERSEVERENCE IS INDEED ATTRACTIVE, MS. PEZZINI..."
WAS THIS BASTARD JUST PLAYING MIND GAMES WITH ME NOW? BACK ON LIBERTY ISLAND, HE SPOKE OF WANTING ME TO SUFFER. WELL, THAT LITTLE PLOY WAS GETTING REALLY OLD WITH ME.
SO WHILE HE WASTED HIS TIME GLARING DOWN ON ME WITH THAT SMUGNESS OF HIS, SEEMINGLY LOOKING FOR GLINTS OF FEAR IN MY EYES TO VALIDATE WHAT-EVER MACHO SHOWMANSHIP HE WAS DISPLAYING, I THOUGHT OF MY PLAN.
KICKING HIM IN THE GROIN HADN'T STOPPED HIM. PERHAPS THE EYES THIS TIME. THOSE GREY EYES.
I MONITORED EVERY SLIGHT MOVEMENT HE MADE. EVERY SHIFT IN STANCE. ANTICIPATING THE WORST. CLEARLY REMEMBERING THAT THIS MAN, DESPITE HIS AIR OF CALM, WAS STILL A MURDERER.
HIS AMBITION TO TAKE MY LIFE HAD BEEN AMONG MY MOST FRIGHTENING MOMENTS EVER. HAD IT NOT BEEN FOR KENNETH IRONS, I'M NOT SO SURE I'D BE ALIVE. IN FACT, I DOUBTED IT.
THEN I FELT HIS BODY TENSE SLIGHTLY. THIS WAS IT.

HE RAISED HIS OPEN HAND. I RECOILED, AS MY MUSCLES TIGHTENED AND MY HEART NEARLY EXPLODED.
NEVER DID I UNTENSE DURING HIS LITTLE CONTROL SCHEME. INSTEAD I MET HIS EYES, HOPING TO MAKE SOME PERSONAL CONNECTION THAT MIGHT'VE MADE IT MORE DIFFICULT FOR HIM TO HURT ME.
I FELT A STING OF EMBARRASSMENT, MY EYES STILL UNCONTROLLABLY FLINCHING, WHEN HIS HAND DIDN'T STRIKE ME AS EXPECTED. AGAIN, THIS GAME OF CONTROL. I COULD ONLY SPECULATE THAT HE ENJOYED TOYING WITH ME.
WHETHER BECAUSE OF MY EYE CONTACT OR SOME OTHER REASON WITHIN HIMSELF, HE BROKE THE SILENCE AGAIN-- WITH A DELUGE OF FACTS.
HE SPOKE OF HAVING A NEED TO TALK TO ME. HE BROUGHT UP LIBERTY ISLAND AND WAS FULL OF FRUSTRATING VAGARIES. HE JUST THREW THINGS OUT THERE WITHOUT PAUSE, NEVER WAITING FOR MY REBUTTAL. HE DIDN'T CARE. I FELT LIKE A PRIEST AT A MOBSTER'S CONFESSIONAL.
I LISTENED LIKE A COP. WAITING FOR THE LIES. BECAUSE IN OUR BUSINESS, EVERYBODY LIES.
HE SPOKE OF THE DREAM HE HAD. AND SURREALISTICALLY I LISTENED WHILE HE RECOUNTED EVERYTHING I HAD DREAMT.

*NOW HE'S TALKING ABOUT THE **RIALTO.** THIS IS JUST TOO MUCH. I DON'T CARE IF HE JUST WANTS TO KILL ME. I NEED SOME ANSWERS... **NOW!***

WHAT ABOUT THE RIALTO? I WANT TO **KNOW!** WHY DON'T YOU TRY TELLING ME AGAIN ABOUT HOW YOU THOUGHT THE WHOLE INCIDENT WAS **INCONVENIENT!** AND WHY STOP **THERE?**

STOP BEING SO VAGUE AND CRYPTIC! TELL ME ABOUT LIBERTY ISLAND! EXPLAIN TO ME WHY I WAS TAKEN ABOARD A **YACHT!**

AND WHILE YOU'RE AT IT, WHAT IS THAT **BRAND** ON YOUR HAND? WHY HAVEN'T YOU **KILLED** ME YET? OR AM I NOT **CONVENIENT** ENOUGHT?!?

TELL ME WHY--!

WHY?

BECCA, WOULD YOU MIND TELLING ME HOW YOU GOT THESE PICTURES?
LOOK, JAKE. I'M CONNECTED. THE PEOPLE THAT HELPED ME GET THESE PHOTOS DON'T WANT TO BE, SO LET'S JUST LEAVE THEM OUT OF THIS.
SO WHAT CONNECTION DOES KENNETH IRONS HAVE WITH THIS NOTTINGHAM GUY?
YOU'RE JOKING, RIGHT? LOOK, I KNOW YOU'RE A COP-- A DETECTIVE AND ALL, BUT THE THING IS--IS THAT KEN IRONS RUNS THE ENTIRE RACKET AND NOTTINGHAM WORKS FOR HIM.
HERE, LOOK-- SEE THE PHOTO. HE'S PAYING OFF A COP! IRONS OWNS ALL OF THEM!
SO, WHAT YOU'RE SAYING IS THAT PUBLIC FIGURE, ENTREPRENEUR, CANCER-FIGHTING, GOOD SAMARITAN KEN IRONS IS SECRETLY INVOLVED WITH THE SOCIETY OF CRIMELORDS AND HIS HENCHMAN IS PAYING OFF COPS?
JAKE? ARE YOU HEARING ME?? WHY SHOULD THAT SURPRISE YOU? NO ONE AT YOUR PRECINCT IS DOING A THING! YOU PROBABLY HAVE A RAT RIGHT UNDER YOUR NOSE!
OKAY, BACK TO THE IRONS EMPIRE. YOU KNOW WHAT? JAKE, WE HAVE REPORTS ON HIM THAT DATE BACK 90 YEARS! OK? HOW IS THAT POSSIBLE? THAT DOESN'T MAKE ANY SENSE. 90 YEARS. LOOK AT HIM. DOES HE LOOK LIKE A 90 YEAR OLD MAN? NO!
THEY COULD HAVE BEEN TALKING ABOUT HIS FATHER.
HIS FATHER IS DEAD. IN FACT, RUMOR HAS IT THAT HE KILLED HIS FATHER IN AN EXCAVATION --BLASTED WITHOUT GIVING ANY WARNING. AS A RESULT, HE WAS CAVED IN.
WELL YOU KNOW WHAT, BECCA, HE'S NOT 90 YEARS OLD--HE'S JUST NOT. HE'S KINDA OLD LOOKING BUT...
WHY CAN'T YOU JUST SEE PAST BLACK AND WHITE? WHY?
BECAUSE I'M A COP. I'VE SEEN A LOT OF WEIRD THINGS, BUT STUFF LIKE THIS--OR WHATEVER YOU'RE TALKING ABOUT--DOESN'T EXIST. IT MAY LOOK UNREAL, BUT FACTS OFTEN GET LOST IN HEARSAY. WE DEAL IN COLD HARD FACTS. WE'RE SCIENTISTS.
JAKE, I HATE TO BREAK IT TO YOU, BUT THE WORLD ISN'T LIKE THAT. THERE'S SO MUCH TO IT THAN YOU REALLY SEE. COP OR NO COP.
SO WHAT'S YOUR FRIEND DOING HANGING OUT WITH KEN IRONS? IS SHE A PROSTITUTE? IS SHE A MODEL? IS SHE STUPID??
JAKE YOU'RE GONNA SKIP HALF YOUR INVESTIGATION IF YOU STICK WITHIN THE BLACK AND WHITE REALM. YOU'VE JUST GOT TO LOOK MORE ABSTRACTLY AT THINGS. OH, AND IF SHE'S WITH KEN IRONS, YOU'RE ALREADY TOO LATE.
HEY! LOOK, YOU CAN'T BLAME HER FOR NOT KNOWING WHAT THE DEAL IS ABOUT HIM. BUT I WANT TO SHOW HER THESE PICTURES. MAYBE THEY'LL WISEN HER UP A LITTLE BIT.

CHELSEA. 10:55 P.M.
GREAT.
NOTICE OF EVICTION
SIX YEARS IN THIS APARTMENT WITHOUT A COMPLAINT. I'M A COUPLE DAYS LATE-- ALL RIGHT, TEN DAYS-- AND THEY'RE TOSSING ME OUT.
LANDLADY DOESN'T CARE WHAT HAPPENS TO ME AS LONG AS SHE GETS MY RENT.
GREAT, JULIE MANAGED TO MAKE HERSELF AT HOME-- FOUND MY LIPSTICK AND VODKA. NICE. PRETTY MUCH SUMS HER UP. I'LL WORRY ABOUT HER LATER.
HEY SIS GUESS
-SIGH- NOW, THINK ABOUT IAN NOTTINGHAM. COULD HE **HAVE** BEEN TELLING THE TRUTH?
DID HE AND KEN REALLY WORK **TOGETHER?** WHAT REALLY HAPPENED ON LIBERTY ISLAND? WAS KEN **REALLY** THERE JUST WATCHING OUT FOR ME? WAS HE REALLY THERE TO **PROTECT** ME?
IF HE KNEW I WAS KIDNAPPED, WHY DIDN'T HE CALL THE POLICE? WHY DIDN'T HE DO **SOMETHING** THEN? DID HE REALLY HAVE MY SAFETY IN MIND?
OKAY. HOLD ON. I GOTTA PIECE THIS TOGETHER. HE MEETS ME AT THE GYM-- I'VE NEVER SEEN HIM THERE BEFORE. HE SEEMS TO FOLLOW--
KNOCK! KNOCK!
HELLOO. PARDON ME SWEETIE, I'M GRACE--A FRIEND OF KENNETH IRONS.
I KNOW THIS MAY SOUND STRANGE, BUT...WELL...KEN IS ATTENDING A CHARITY I HELPED ORGANIZED AND HE WAS HOPING YOU'D JOIN HIM.
I KNOW IT'S SHORT NOTICE, SO HE HAD ME PICK UP SOMETHING FOR YOU TO WEAR.
WELL...
YOU SEE, EVER SINCE HIS EX-WIFE, DANNI DIED, HE'S JUST BEEN SO SHY AND WELL--HE PICKED OUT THIS NECKLACE FOR YOU AND...
...HERE, LET'S GET YOU INTO THIS. HE'LL BE SO **HAPPY**!

11:10P.M.
-SIGH- OK--
-AHEM- SARA, WE NEED TO TALK.
NO. NO, SHE'LL THINK--SHE'LL WANT TO AVOID ANY CONVERSATION THAT STARTS LIKE THAT.
OKAY. AS A CLOSE FRIEND AND CO-WORKER--I'D LIKE TO TALK TO YOU ABOUT KENNETH IRONS. HMM. SARA, I WANT TO TALK TO YOU ABOUT KEN IRONS--THE GUY YOU'VE BEEN SEEING.
NO, THAT MAKES ME SOUND LIKE A JEALOUS BOYFRIEND. MAN, I WISH I COULD JUST TALK TO HER ALONE AGAIN AND GET HOW WE FEEL ABOUT EACH OTHER ON THE TABLE. I'M PRETTY SURE SHE LIKES ME...
OKAY, SARA, THE GUY YOU'VE BEEN SEEING IS A CROOK--AND WILL KILL YOU. YEAH, RIGHT. LIKE I CAN SAY THAT. DAMN, THERE DOESN'T SEEM TO BE ANY DECENT WAY TO--WHOA!!
WHERE'S SHE GOING? JEEZ, SARA, WHAT THE HELL YOU DOING DRESSED UP LIKE THAT?
IRONS--9? GREAT. LOOKS LIKE YOU'RE GOING SOMEWHERE. AREN'T YOU, SARA?
IRONS 9
WELL, ME TOO.

HE RIVERDALE COMPOUND. OME OF THE CHURCH OF OLY PROSPERITY. 11:40P.M.
I NEVER THOUGHT I'D STEP FOOT IN THIS PLACE. FOR SOME REASON, I'VE ALWAYS STAYED AWAY FROM RELIGIONS THAT BASE THEIR FOUNDATION ON CLEVER SLOGANS LIKE, "YOUR SPIRIT IS OUR BUSINESS."
MAYBE IT'S ME, BUT A BELIEF IN GOD SHOULDN'T BE BASED ON HOW MUCH MONEY YOU HAVE. THAT'S JUST MY OPINION.
BUT IF BEING HERE WITH KEN HELPS RAISE MONEY FOR A CURE FOR CANCER--I CAN CERTAINLY PUT AWAY MY DIFFERENCES. IN FACT, IT'LL BE A GOOD CHANGE OF SCENERY.
...MR IRONS, WE'RE QUITE INSPIRED THAT YOU COULD MAKE OUR BENEFIT TONIGHT.
YES, ALL THE FELLOW PROSPERITES HAVE FOUND YOUR APPEARANCE QUITE INSPIRATIONAL.
OF COURSE, MY FRIENDS. AFTER PERUSING YOUR RECENT RESEARCH, I BELIEVE YOUR THEORIES ON CANCER TO BE REFRESHING.
WHY, I'M FLATTERED, MR. IR--
PARDON ME...
...BUT I BELIEVE MY GUEST HAS ARRIVED.

HOW INSPIRING.
OOOH...
OH, MOM, IF YOU COULD SEE ME NOW. THE ATTENTION IS ON **ME**--AND IT'S IN A **GOOD** WAY!
NO WOMAN IS JEALOUSLY WHISPERING IN FRONT OF ME. AND THE MEN, THEY AREN'T LEERING AT ME. THEY LOOK--THEY LOOK GENUINELY **HAPPY** TO SEE ME.
THEIR BELIEFS **MAY** BE OFF BASE, BUT THIS IS THE FIRST TIME--I MEAN--THEY'RE SO **NICE** TO ME. UNLIKE THE PEOPLE I **NORMALLY** ASSOCIATE WITH, **THESE** KNOW THE DIFFERENCE BETWEEN **GIVENCHY** AND **GARANIMALS!**
MAYBE THE GRASS **IS** GREENER, MOM.

THIS IS HOW I SHOULD LOOK--HOW I SHOULD FEEL. IT JUST SEEMS SO RIGHT TO BE WEARING SOMETHING SO SOFT--SO CARESSING TO MY SKIN. IT MAKES ME FEEL...SO BEAUTIFUL.
IT DOESN'T CONFINE MY BODY LIKE THE WITCHBLADE DOES. IT'S NOT BRUISING ME. NOR DO I BELIEVE THAT WHEN I TAKE IT OFF, WILL IT RESIST LIKE THE WITCHBLADE DID.
AND THIS PEARL NECKLACE--MUCH BETTER ON MY NECK THAN BULLETS.
I FEEL SAFE. I FEEL GOOD.
MOMMY, WHO'S THAT BEAUTIFUL LADY?

SARA. YOU'VE MADE **QUITE** AN IMPRESSION.
GRACE TOLD ME THAT SHE WENT TO YOUR HOUSE TO FIND YOU. I--I FEEL HONORED YOU CHOSE TO COME.
I DIDN'T KNOW HOW TO ASK YOU AND WELL, SHE'S LIKE A MUM TO ME--
I WOULD HAVE NEVER TAKEN YOU FOR THE **SHY** TYPE. I'M **GLAD** SHE TOOK THE REINS. AND I'M GLAD I'M HERE WITH YOU.
OH WILLIAM, ISN'T SHE JUST **STUNNING!**
INDEED, GRACE. SHE IS TRULY **PROSPERITE** MATERIAL.
BESIDES, HOW **COULD** I PASS UP A BENEFIT AT THE FAMOUS **RIVERDALE COMPOUND?**
ITS REAL NAME IS THE *"ENLIGHTENMENT CENTER"*. IT'S REALLY NOT A *"COMPOUND"*. **BUT--** NEVER MIND THAT--LET'S GET OUT OF THIS **CROWD** YOU'VE CREATED AND MINGLE, SHALL WE?

I'M NOT SURE I UNDERSTAND. AND ISN'T THIS KINDA LATE FOR A GATHERING? ESPECIALLY WITH ALL THESE KIDS--?
YOU KNOW HIM?
AH, MICHAEL.
WELL, I AM A BIT CONNECTED. ~CHUCKLE~ LET'S SEE IF I CAN MANAGE AN INTRODUCTION.
WHAT'S UP, KENNY?
KENNY?
THIS IS TOO COOL!
I WON'T TELL HIM ABOUT THAT "MR. BLONDE" POSTER ON MY WALL. HE'D THINK I WAS A GEEK

MIKE, YOU NOW HAVE THE PRIVILEGE TO MEET MY GUEST. DETECTIVE SARA PEZZINI.
BEHAVE AROUND HER OR I SHALL HAVE THE BARTENDER SEND YOU A TAB OF ALL THOSE DRINKS YOU'VE BEEN GUZZLING.
WHAT ARE YOU DRINKING, MISS PEZZINI?
SARA, IF YOU DON'T FIND MICHAEL'S MANNER TOO, SHALL WE SAY COARSE, I WONDER IF YOU'D EXCUSE ME FOR A MOMENT?
MAYBE I HAD IT ALL WRONG...
SOOO, ARE YOU A PROSPERITE?
NO, BUT MY SISTER ONCE WENT TO ONE OF THEIR CONVENTIONS IN LOS ANGELES. SHE SAID SHE WAS SWORN TO SECRECY.
ARE YOU??
SWORN TO SECRECY? ALWAYS. HEH. NO, I'M NOT A MEMBER PER SE. THEY HAVE GREAT PARTIES, THOUGH, HUH?
YEAH.
...I COULD GET USED TO THIS.
AND FUNNY IDEAS. IF YOU GET A CHANCE, ASK 'EM ABOUT THEIR CURE FOR CAN--
SARA!!
NO, NO, NO, NO, NO, NO!
WE NEED TO TALK!
JAKE... HOW DID YOU GET IN? DID YOU SNEAK IN HERE?

--SARA C'MON! THIS IS NO TIME TO BE PICKING UP ON--LOOK, I HAVE TO SHOW YOU SOMETHING.
UGGH-- WHAT ARE YOU DOING AT A PLACE LIKE THIS?
IT'S NONE OF YOUR BUSINESS, JAKE!
WELL IT IS IF IT HAS TO DO WITH KENNETH IRONS. THE MAN'S A MURDERER, SARA--A CRIMELORD. HE WAS THE HEAD OF THE RIALTO MURD-- J-JUST TAKE A LOOK AT THESE PHOTOS!
*COUGH* UH-YEAH, I'LL JUST LEAVE YOU TWO LOVEBIRDS ALONE.
MAYBE WE CAN FINISH UP THAT STORY SOME OTHER TIME.
I DON'T WANT TO LOOK AT YOUR STUPID TABLOID PICTURES JAKE! YOU'RE RUINING MY TIME!
WHAP!
DID YOU FOLLOW ME HERE?
SARA, IT WAS ONLY FOR YOUR PROTECTION!
MY? MY PROTECTION? FROM WHAT? JAKE, GET OUT! AND STOP STALKING ME.
REALLY JAKE, I NEVER EXPECTED THIS OF YOU. YOU CAN'T EVEN PULL OFF STALKING PROPERLY. HAVEN'T YOU GOT ANYTHING BETTER TO DO?
SARA, YOU'RE IN DANGER!
SIR, I'M GOING TO HAVE TO ASK YOU TO--
DON'T BOTHER! I'M LEAVIN' ANYWAY!
JAKE, I'M CALLING SECURITY.
ON ME?? SARA, YOU'VE LOST IT! YOU DON'T WANT MY HELP, THAT'S ALL YOU NEEDED TO SAY! BUT THIS MAN'S GOING TO KILL YOU. YOU HEAR ME? FINE!

SOON...
KEN? KEN, IT'S BEEN AN HOUR. PLEASE SAY SOMETHING. I-I CAN'T STAND THIS SILENCE.
I'M UH--I'M NOT DATING HIM. HE WORKS WITH ME.
WHY WON'T YOU TALK TO ME? IF THIS IS ABOUT JAKE, I-I'M SORRY.
RRRRIGHT. THERE'S NOTHING TO DISCUSS. THE NIGHT IS OVER. I'LL DROP YOU OFF AT YOUR APARTMENT.
NO! I-I WANT TO TALK ABOUT THIS. YOU JUST CAN'T SHUT ME OUT LIKE THIS! YOU CAN'T. THIS IS JUST--IT'S JUST A MISUNDERSTANDING.
DID HE SAY ANYTHING TO YOU? DID HE SAY SOMETHING ABOUT ME?
SARA, YOUR ACTIONS SPEAK WELL ENOUGH FOR YOU. AND I DON'T WANT TO TALK ANYMORE ABOUT THIS. YOU MIGHT WANT TO MAKE A NOTE OF THAT BECAUSE THIS IS GETTING BORING NOW.
BORING? WHAT? NOTHING HAPPENED! WHAT ARE YOU TALKING ABOUT? I'M CONFUSED KEN, PLEASE HELP ME KNOW WHAT I DID WRONG.
I SAID-- END OF DISCUSSION. I'M DONE.
WELL, I'M NOT! KEN, YOU DON'T UNDERSTAND. JUST GIVE ME A CHANCE TO EXPLAIN.
SARA, STOP PLAYING GAMES. I DON'T WANT TO TALK ABOUT THIS IN THE CAR. JUST BE QUIET OK? YOU'RE MAKING MY HEAD HURT.
IRONS 1

WHAAAM!
DAMN!!
"HAVEN'T YOU GOT ANYTHING BETTER TO DO?" UNGH--NO! I DON'T, SARA! SORRY I CARE ABOUT YOU! BUT DON'T WORRY--I WON'T BOTHER YOU ANYMORE.
MMPH-- I JUST WANNA--
JAKE-- YOU ALL RIGHT?
...I... I'M... FINE.
AAALRIGHT... WELL...MAYBE YOU SHOULD WATCH THE CAFFEINE, THEN.
THIS HAVE TO DO WITH SARA? SHE ALL RIGHT?
..YOU KNOW, CHIEF, SHE'S DOING GREAT, DAMMIT.
SO GREAT, IN FACT, THAT SHE DOESN'T NEED ANY HELP FROM ME. EVER!
...OKAY, JAKE. MAYBE I'LL JUST GIVE HER A CALL...
WHATEVER. LATER, CHIEF.

HAVING GIRL TROUBLES, JAKE?
DON'T WORRY. MAYBE IRONS WON'T BE ABLE TO GET IT UP.
YOU KNOW WHAT, SELZER? YOU--YOU? IRONS? ...SELZER, YOU AND I ARE GONNA HAVE A LITTLE TALK. NOW.

YOU SAID YOU DIDN'T WANT TO TALK IN THE CAR. WELL, WE'RE HERE.
KEN?
AND HOW THE HELL DO YOU KNOW WHAT I'M THINKING!!?!!!
-GASP!- K--
DID YOU ONCE THINK ABOUT HOW YOU MADE A COMPLETE FOOL OF ME BY CAUSING THAT FIASCO??
DID YOU ONCE REMEMBER WHO I AM TO THE COMMUNITY AND PUBLIC EYE?
I APOLOGIZE FOR JAKE. HE--HE FOLLOWED ME. I'M SORRY!
IS THAT WHAT'S BOTHERING YOU? I'M SORRY. IF HE SAID SOMETHING TO YOU ABOUT ME --IT'S NOT TRUE!
IT'S--IT'S NOT WHAT YOU THINK.

DID YOU FORGET THAT WE WERE AT A FUND-RAISER WITH DECENT PEOPLE? NOT WITH CRIMINALS LIKE YOU DEAL WITH!
KEN--PLEASE--STOP...
THAT WAS MY EVENT--TO HELP OTHERS AND ALL YOU CAN DO IS THROW A FIT IN FRONT OF EVERYBODY.
DON'T INTERRUPT ME! THE EVENT WAS A FAILURE BECAUSE OF YOU AND YOUR LITTLE JEALOUS BOYFRIEND ANTICS!
KEN, I WASN'T THAT LOUD. ONLY A FEW PEOPLE SAW--
DO YOU THINK I'M GOING TO BE ANOTHER JAKE? DO YOU THINK YOU CAN PULL MY PUPPET STRINGS???
KEN PLEASE. -GASP!- OOWW. THAT'S NOT WHAT I THINK. PLEASE STOP YELLING AT ME--PLEASE. OOHH.
I DIDN'T KNOW SOMETHING LIKE THAT WOULD UPSET YOU SO MUCH I-I DON'T EVEN REALLY KNOW YOU--
YOU'RE BLEEDING SARA. YOU SEE?? YOU'RE BAD AND THE WITCHBLADE IS PUNISHING YOU.
NNOO, I DIDN'T DO ANYTHING, OOWW -SOB-
-SOB- OWW. KEN? TELL ME! -SOB- YOU'RE TALKING ABOUT SO MANY THINGS. I DON'T UNDERSTAND. THIS CAN'T BE HAPPENING!

CAN'T BE **HAPPENING?** SCHOPENHAUER ONCE SAID "WHAT MOST PEOPLE COMMONLY CALL **FATE** IS MOSTLY THEIR OWN **STUPIDITIES!**" THIS **IS** HAPPENING.
I BELIEVE SHE'S **READY** FOR YOU NOW, MR. NOTTINGHAM.

# ISSUE #8

story: **David Wohl** and **Christina Z.**
pencils and co-plot: **Michael Turner**
inks: **D-Tron**
colors: **JD Smith**

IT'S TOO LATE. I'LL TAKE YOU TO MEET HIM, BUT SARA'S ALREADY DEAD.
YOU CAN'T PROVE IT, EITHER. SARA FELL FOR HIS PUPPET SHOW JUST LIKE EVERYBODY ELSE, TURNING HER INTO A FAILURE BY PITTING ALL HER WEAKNESSES AGAINST HER. IT WAS PLANNED FROM DAY ONE, OR RATHER, THE RIALTO.
JAKE-- DO YOU KNOW WHAT HAPPENED TO SARA AT THE RIALTO?
CLICK!
I DON'T CARE! JUST SHUT UP AND DRIVE.
HEY, OK. YOU WANNA MEET THE MAN, YOU GOT IT. I CAN'T WAIT TO SEE THE LOOK ON YOUR MOTHER'S FACE WHEN SHE HAS TO IDENTIFY YOUR BODY. I'LL TRY NOT TO LAUGH.
HE PITTED HER WEAKNESSES AGAINST HER? WHAT ARE YOU--
OH, YOU REALLY KNOW A LOT ABOUT SARA, DON'T YOU? WHO DO YOU THINK OFFERED HER ALL THE ANSWERS TO WHAT'S HAPPENED TO HER? WHAT OTHER PERSON COULD TELL HER ABOUT THE WITCHBLADE??
--THE WHA--??
WHO BUT IRONS COULD PUT ORDER BACK INTO HER LIFE? YOUR POOR SARA'SBEEN THROUGH A LOT MORE THAN YOU WILL EVER KNOW AND IT'S REALLY TOO BAD THAT ALL THIS TIME SHE THOUGHT HE WAS TRYING TO HELP HER!
HELL, I'M PROUD TO INTRODUCE YOU TO KEN IRONS, MY BOSS.

CAUTY TOWER. CENTRAL PARK WEST, NEW YORK. 4:25 A.M.
FRUSTRATION.
A STABBING, HOT, AGONIZING FRUSTRATION.
JUST TOO MANY EVENTS, ONE RIGHT AFTER ANOTHER, LEADING TO THIS-- THE PINNACLE OF DESPAIR
SHE WANTED QUICK ANSWERS--AN EASY RESOLUTION.
SHE EVEN BELIEVED, FOR A FLEETING MOMENT, THAT SHE COULD LIVE THE GLAMOROUS LIFESTYLE SHE ONCE LONGED FOR.
NOW SHE'S ALONE.
SARA, DO YOU REALLY THINK I JUST HAPPENED TO STUMBLE UPON YOU AT LIBERTY ISLAND?
COULD NOT A CLEVER DETECTIVE LIKE YOURSELF REALIZE THAT THE SLIP FROM WHICH MY YACHT WAS DOCKED, WAS INDEED REGISTERED UNDER MY NAME?
I DO THINK MANY OF YOUR COLLEAGUES COULD LEARN FROM YOUR CARELESS-NESS.
SHE KNOWS SHE MUST DEAL WITH THIS ON HER OWN--WITHOUT THE WITCHBLADE.
I'M SORRY--OR WERE THERE TOO MANY OTHER THOUGHTS RACING THROUGH THAT COMPLEX MIND OF YOURS? YOUR PARTNER, MICHAEL YEE, PERHAPS? WHAT WITH HIS UNTIMELY AND INCONVENIENT DEATH, IT'S NO WONDER!
THAT GAUNTLET FORSOOK HER LONG AGO.
PERHAPS THERE WAS MORE, TOO. I DON'T BLAME YOU FOR SLIPPING UP, SARA. IT WAS SURELY A SHOCK TO YOUR SYSTEM--THE DISASTER AT THE RIALTO, YOUR KID-NAPPING FROM THE GYM-- MAYBE TRYING TO RESURRECT MICHAEL WAS A LITTLE MORE THAN YOU SHOULD HAVE ATTEMPTED.

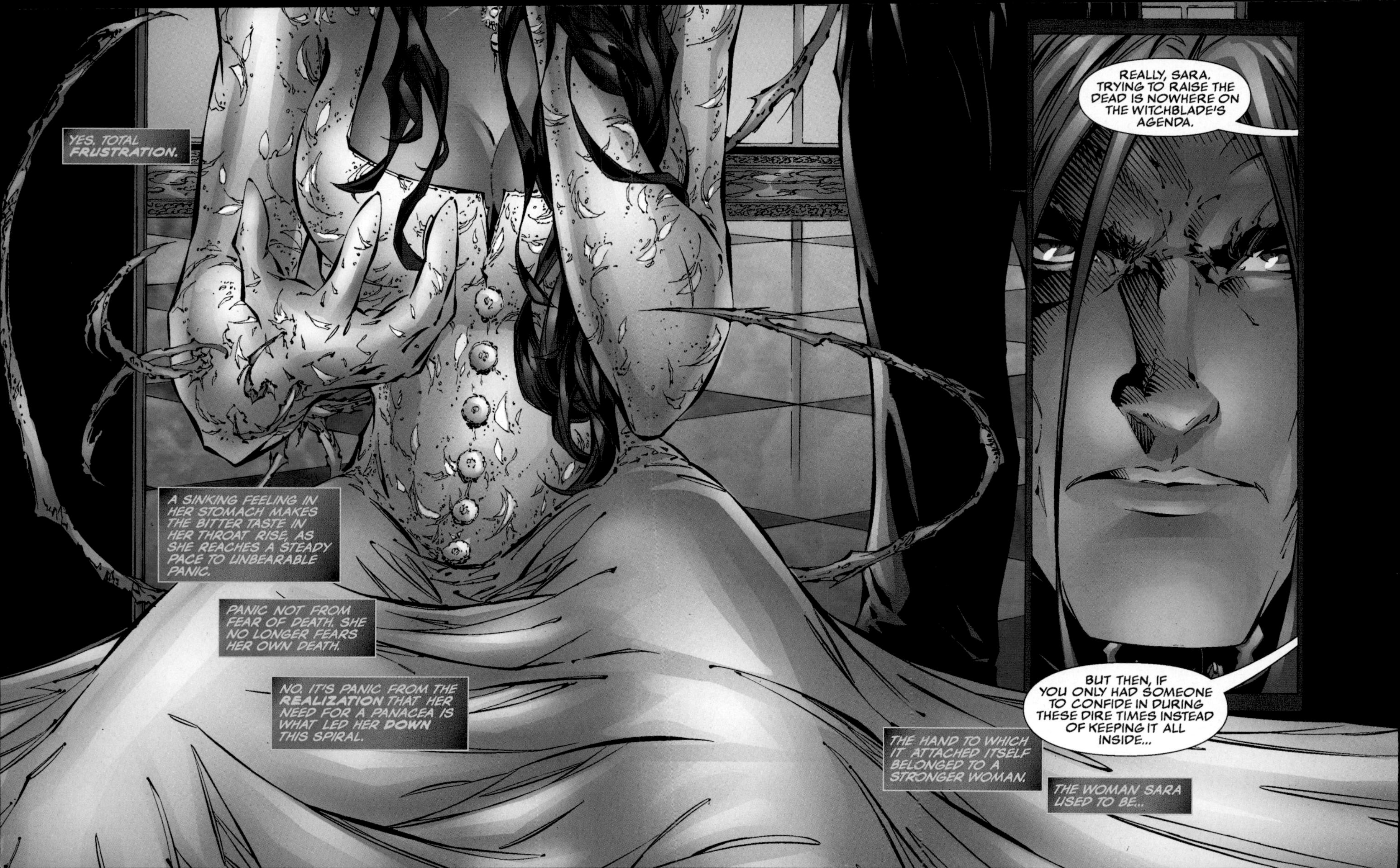
YES, TOTAL **FRUSTRATION.**
A SINKING FEELING IN HER STOMACH MAKES THE BITTER TASTE IN HER THROAT RISE, AS SHE REACHES A STEADY PACE TO UNBEARABLE PANIC.
PANIC NOT FROM FEAR OF DEATH. SHE NO LONGER FEARS HER OWN DEATH.
NO, IT'S PANIC FROM THE **REALIZATION** THAT HER NEED FOR A PANACEA IS WHAT LED HER **DOWN** THIS SPIRAL.
REALLY, SARA. TRYING TO RAISE THE DEAD IS NOWHERE ON THE WITCHBLADE'S AGENDA.
BUT THEN, IF YOU ONLY HAD SOMEONE TO CONFIDE IN DURING THESE DIRE TIMES INSTEAD OF KEEPING IT ALL INSIDE...
THE HAND TO WHICH IT ATTACHED ITSELF BELONGED TO A STRONGER WOMAN.
THE WOMAN SARA USED TO BE...

...BEHIND THESE THOUGHTS, SHE HEARS IRONS--HIS VOICE LIKE AN ECHO THROUGH A TUNNEL. SHE KNOWS SHE SHOULD BE LISTENING, THINKING, PLANNING--BUT SHE CAN'T.
EVERYTHING BEGINS TO FOCUS, BUT IT'S TOO LATE, NOW.
I BELIEVE THAT'S WHAT YOU WANTED FROM ME, WAS IT NOT? I RECALL, THERE WAS A DEFINITE SPARK IN THOSE EYES WHEN WE FIRST MET--A CERTAIN DESIRE YOU WANTED QUENCHED BY ME, YES?
I'LL ALWAYS WONDER WHY THE WITCHBLADE CHOSE YOU. YOU SEEM FAR TOO YOUNG-- TOO UNGROOMED FOR IT'S GRANDEUR.
KKRRASSSSH!
NOTTINGHAM SPENT YEARS BEING MODIFIED FOR SUCH A TIME THAT HE MIGHT WIELD IT. YET, ON LIBERTY ISLAND, ITS INTENSITY DROVE HIM TO THE BRINK OF INSANITY--
--AS IT WAS INTENDED THAT HE FILTER THE NEGATIVE RESIDUE, RENDERING IT BENIGN ENOUGH FOR ME TO CONTROL ITS RAW ENERGY.
AND SINCE YOU'VE BECOME LESS THAN WHAT IT REQUIRES OF YOU--IT WILL BE EASIER TO TRANSFER. I MUST THANK YOU FOR THAT.
NOTTINGHAM-- BEGIN THE CEREMONY!!
IAN-- WAIT--
R-REMEMBER OUR DREAM. IAN, DON'T HURT ME. PLEASE. I KNOW YOU CARE--DON'T YOU?
NO.

OH, AND DID YOU KNOW--
SSHIINKK!
...THAT THOSE HANDS WHICH WILL TAKE YOUR LIFE, SHALL PLAY A CONCIERTO ON THE BÖSENDORFER WHEN YOU'RE DEAD?
IRONIC, ISN'T IT?
--THOSE WHO LIVE ON HOPE ALONE, DEAR GIRL, WILL DIE STARVING!!
HAHA HAH--
STUNNED SILENT THAT HER ATTEMPT TO CONNECT WITH NOTTINGHAM GENERATES NO RESULT, THE PLEA EMANATES IN HER MIND:
I--I HAVE HOPE. I HAVE HOPE YOU WON'T HURT... I--I HAVE HO--

HAHAouuu!
WHAMM!
YOU-
KOFF
BETRAY--
ME??
HOW
DARE
YOU!!
AAGGHH!
NOOOO!

HOW QUICKLY YOU FORGET WHO I AM! I AM NOT YOUR ASSASSIN! I AM NOT YOUR LOYAL SERVANT. I WOULD HAVE GIVEN MY LIFE FOR YOU, BUT FOREMOST--
--I WAS A CONFIDANT!!
AND IT IS NOT WISE TO REMOVE A FLY FROM A FRIEND'S FOREHEAD WITH A HATCHET!!
YOU HAVE BETRAYED ME!
N-NOTTINGHAM --GGL--DGGLL-- KLL-MUHH...
SHHINNN!

NNNNN
UGGH!! YOU TRIED THIS ONCE BEFORE AND FAILED, DID YOU NOT?
I AM THRICE YOUR AGE, BOY. AND I HAVE LEARNED THAT AS MAN GETS ANGRY--
--HE FALLS INTO--
ERROR!!

YOU STUPID, INSOLENT DOLT! YOU WERE NOT BETRAYED! IT WAS YOUR DUTY TO KEEP ME FROM HARM. YOU ARE INSUBORDINATE AND I WILL ENJOY HURTING YOU!
AS ALWAYS, I AM HAPPY TO TEACH YOU...
...NGGG-- A LESSON!
KRAAKK!
OH GOD..
SARA! --I HOPE...
KRRAAKK!
...YOU'RE PAYING ATTENTION SINCE THIS IS YOUR FAULT. WITH EVERY...
KRRAAKK!
...BLOW I BESTOW UPON HIM...
...HE'S PAYING FOR YOUR SINS--
--AND HIS SICKENING SYMPATHY FOR YOU!
AAGH!
TELL ME, IAN. TELL ME YOU ENJOY PROTECTING THIS WOMAN! TELL ME YOUR LOYALTY LIES WITH HER!

WELL, SARA, REGARDLESS OF YOUR "RENDEZVOUS," HE WOULDN'T HAVE REMAINED LOYAL LONG-- IAN NEEDS A TYPE OF DISCIPLINE YOU COULD NEVER UNDERSTAND.
OH, IAN, YOU'RE QUITE A MESS AND MOST CERTAINLY...
...USELESS TO ME!
KRAASSHH!
NOW...
...LET'S SEE IF WE CAN ADJUST THAT ATTITUDE OF YOURS. NOTTINGHAM MAY HAVE BEEN AGAINST PROLONGED TORTURE. I'M NOT!
I DON'T HAVE TO TELL YOU AGAIN-- I FOUND IT--IT WAS MY TOURNAMENT AT THE RIALTO--AND I WANT IT BACK!
YOUR TOURNAMENT?
NO WONDER YOU KNEW ALL ABOUT ME.
YOU HAD ME TRAILED THE WHOLE TIME?

THINKING BACK TO THAT NIGHT AND FORMING THE WORDS ON HER LIPS, HER VOICE CRACKS.
I TRIED THAT ONCE.
AND IT DIDN'T WORK!
SINCE THEN, I'VE REFINED MY METHODS.
TAKE IT THEN.
TAKE IT!
NOTTINGHAM WOULD HAVE BEEN HELPFUL...
...BUT HE'S NO LONGER NECESSARY.
YEEEEA
EESSSSS!

THE POWER ENGULFS HIS BODY, SHAKING HIS ENTIRE BEING FROM THE INSIDE, OUT.
HEART BEATING AT AN INCALCULABLE RATE AS HE FEELS AN INTERNAL WIND TUNNEL READY TO BURST OUTWARD.
THEN THE THOUGHTS FORCE THEIR WAY, CONNECTING SYNAPSE TO NERVE THROUGH BLOOD AND MUSCLE--THEY FORGE A PATH INTO HIS BRAIN, THREATENING TO PULL HIS SANITY FROM HIM.
BUT HE HOLDS TIGHT TO IT. BARELY.
I AM MASTER!
I AM POWER!!

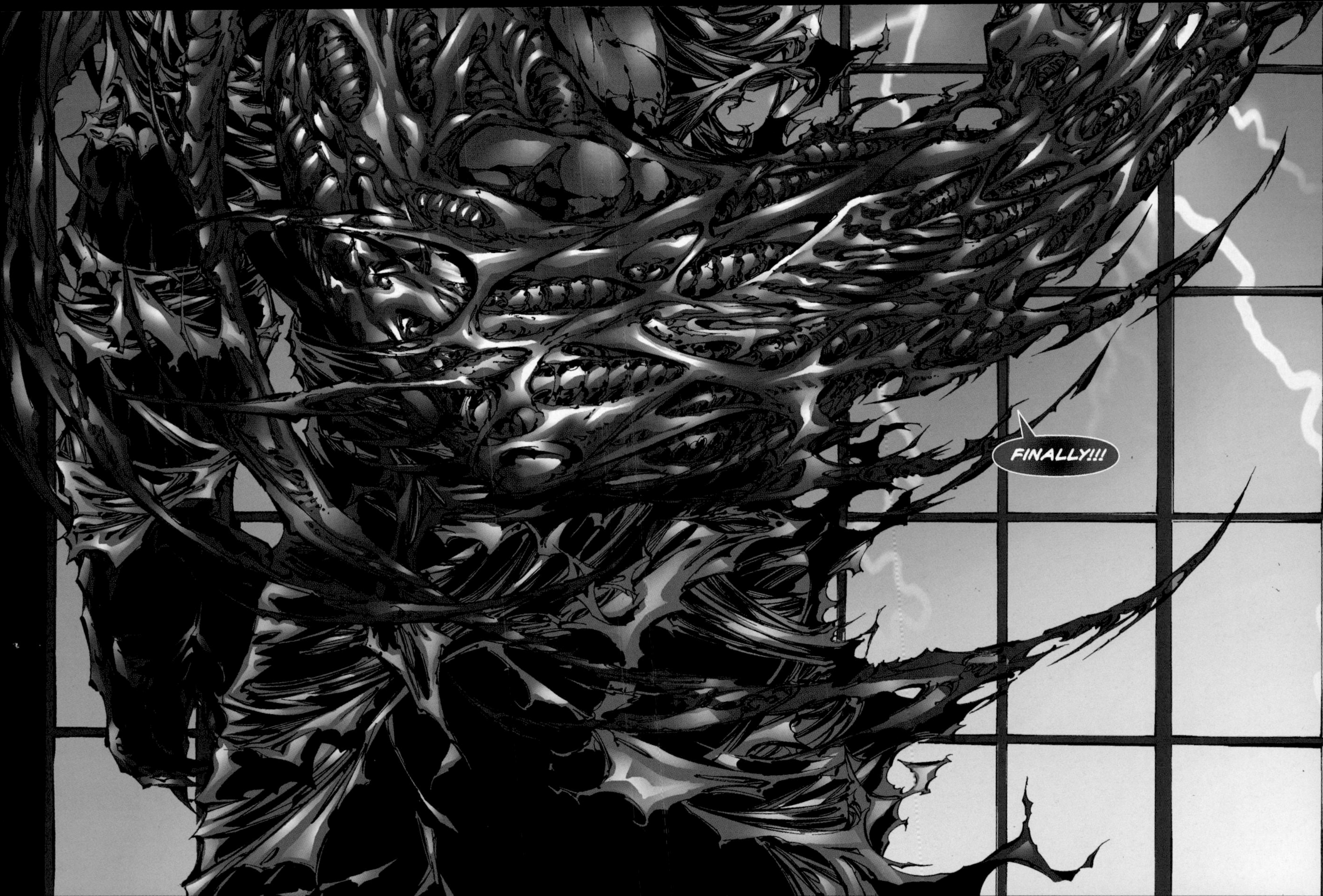
FINALLY!!!

BOSS!--
HEY, LOOK
WHO'S HERE.
B--BOSS?!?
WHAT IS
THIS?
NNNGG--YOU!!!
I WANT THE REST
OF IT!!! GIVE IT
TO ME!!
I--NEED--
GGZZAMMM
DEAR
GOD IN
HEAVEN.
I
AM
GOD!!!
BLAM!
BLAM! BLAM!
NOT FOR
LONG!!
SARA,
TAKE COVER!!
I SAID
GO!!
IT WOULD BE EASY.
SHE HAS NO WEAPON.
BUT IT'S CLEAR WHAT
HER PURPOSE IS.
YES.
CHINK!
CHINK!
CHINK!
VVZZZ!
BECAUSE ABOVE ALL
ELSE, SHE IS A COP.
AND HAS TAKEN AN
OATH TO PROTECT.
I AM
HERE TO--
DESTROY!!
UUGGH!
I AM--

...HERE TO PROTECT!!
I'M NOT GOING TO LET YOU TAKE ANOTHER LIF--
VVVZZZTTTT!
GO AWAY!
PAIN SHOOTS THROUGH HER HEART, JARRING IT TO BEAT, RESUSCITATING HER AS SHE HEARS WORDS THAT NEARLY ECHO THE SAME AS--
LEAVE HER ALONE! KILL ME!
GET IT OVER WITH!!
MICHAEL, NO!!!

KEERRASHH!
SARA!!!
NO!
BLAM! BLAM!
I WON'T LET THIS HAPPEN AGAIN. EVER!
KEESHH!
NOTTINGHAM WAS RIGHT.
SHE HOPES NO MORE--
--BUT TAKES ACTION INSTEAD.
WNRRLSSH!
BODY AND SPIRIT BECOME ONE. BECOME CLEAR. BECOME FOCUSED. BECOME UNITED.
I AM ALMIGHTY!!
HEY!--
HNN?

IT'S SO EASY TO BE ALMIGHTY FROM A DISTANCE, ISN'T IT?

LET'S GO!

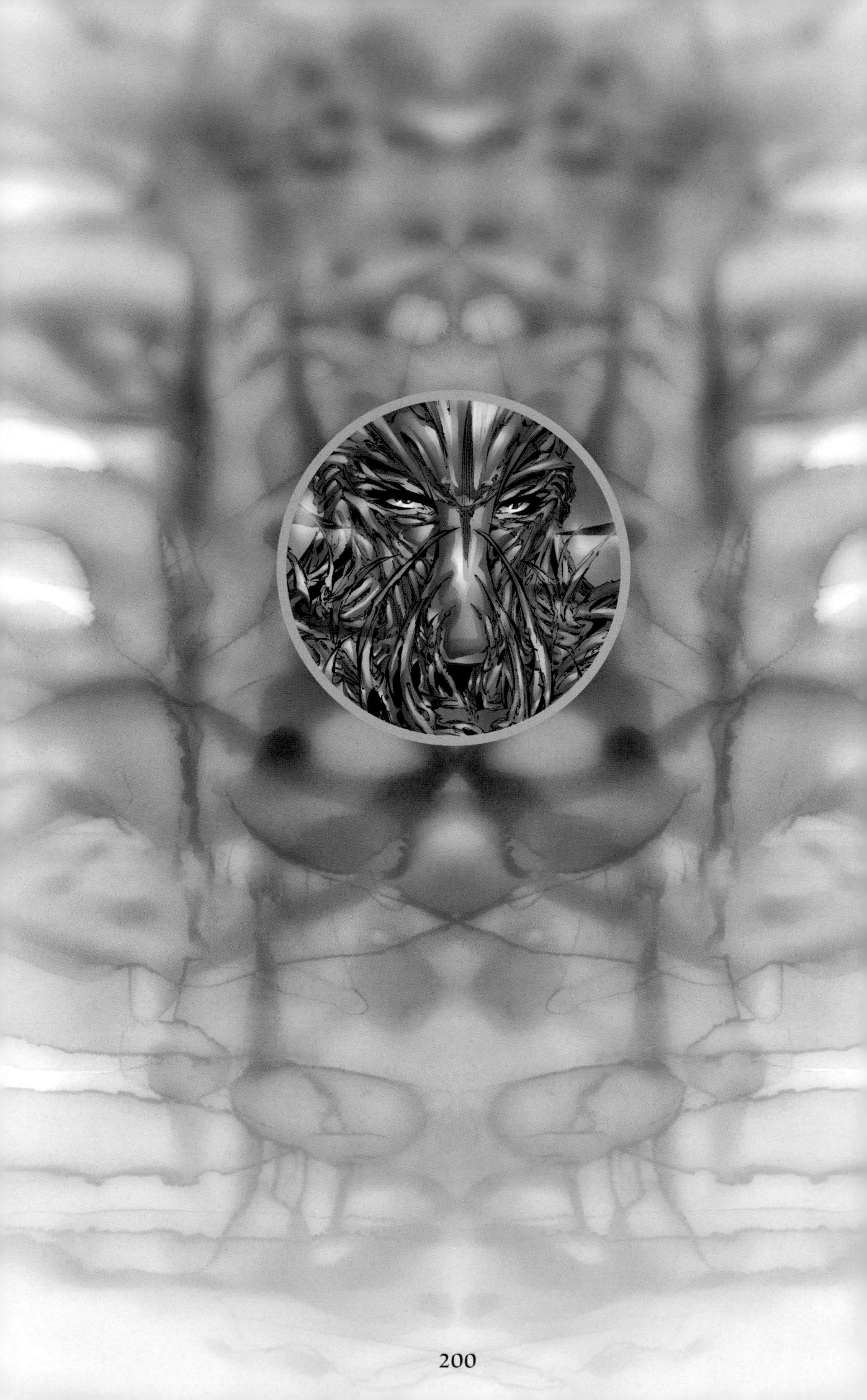

I'LL BE WITH YOU IN A MOMENT.
WZZGGGTT!
NO, BRING IT ON RIGHT NOW!
IT'S THIS THAT YOU WANT.
LOOK AT ME! IT OBEYS ME!!!
YOU'RE SO STUPID. YOU OF ALL PEOPLE--HOW COULD YOU NOT KNOW--WITH YOUR GALLERY--
--THE ONE THING THEY ALL HAD IN COMMON--
--THE WITCHBLADE ONLY CHOOSES WOMEN!!
NNNO!! YOU DON'T KNOW! YOU NEED ME TO TELL YOU!! YOU NEED MY HELP!
NOT ANY MORE!
THMMP!

THE WITCHBLADE MAY GO WITH OTHERS...
...THE INSECURE-- NEVER!!
COOL.
AS IT WAS MEANT FOR ONLY A SPECIFIC WIELDER--ATTACHING NOT ONLY TO BODY, BUT SOUL. AND TO HER SOUL, IT CLINGS.
TO HIS, IT DISEASES.

WHO'S INSECURE??
I'M JUST TAKING BACK WHAT BELONGS TO ME.
THWIPP!
NO.
WHAPP!
YOU'RE NOTHING BUT A LOSER.
AND YOU'LL NEVER HURT ANYONE AGAIN!!
NOOO!!
I-- I'VE FAILED.
YES YOU DID, BUT NOW YOU'RE UNDER ARREST. GET UP.

I-I--
I MUST HAVE IT!
IT'S MY RIGHT!
DON'T BE SO SURE OF YOUR-SELF IRONS! IT'S WHAT LED YOU INTO TROUBLE THE FIRST TIME!
YOUR EMPIRE WILL CRUMBLE WHEN THE WORLD FINDS OUT ABOUT YOU.
YOU CAN'T DO THIS TO ME! I AM A BUSINESSMAN! KILL ME INSTEAD!
I WILL BE REMEMBERED AS THE CRUELEST PLAYER ON THE PLANET, ANYWAY!!
RRRRRIIIGHT. WE ARE ALL AWARE OF THAT--

CRUELTY TYPICALLY ORIGINATES FROM A VILE MIND AND A COWARDLY HEART. YOU'RE THROUGH, IRONS. GIVE UP OR SUFFER.
KILL ME SARA, DO IT!!
WITH HIS WORDS, SHE FEELS IT --THE WITCHBLADE. CONNECTING IN HER MIND. IT'S FULL ENERGY, MAKING HER TREMBLE, AS IT IMPLORES HER TO UNLEASH ITS NATURAL CALLING.
PAIN LAYS ITS TOUCH NOT UPON A CORPSE, SARA. KILL ME. SHOW ME THE ESSENCE OF THE WITCHBLADE. SHOW ME YOUR POWER.
NO. YOU DON'T DESERVE IT. SURRENDER NOW.
WE WILL DESTROY HIM.
NO. NO, WE WON'T.
AND SO NOW, SHE UNDERSTANDS HERSELF. HER SURVIVAL ALL ALONG WAS HER OWN. THE WITCHBLADE-- AN ALLY.
EVEN IF I DID, KNOW THAT I WAS NOT THE ONLY ONE LOOKING FOR YOU. YOU'LL FIND OUT.
KILL ME!!
THAT WOULD BE TOO EASY.
THEN--ONE SHOULD DIE PROUDLY WHEN IT IS NO LONGER POSSIBLE TO LIVE PROUDLY. DEATH LEVELS ALL THINGS.
NO. IT DOESN'T. YOU DIE A COWARD, IRONS.

IT IS ALWAYS DARKEST BEFORE SUNRISE.
WITH SWEET STRENGTH, WITH NEW VISION, SHE SPEAKS TO THE GOLDEN MYSTERY OF DAWN AND TO THE WORLD.
I AM THE LIGHT.
AN ANGEL OF LIFE.
I AM POWER.
I AM MORE THAN HE THOUGHT I'D BE.
S-SARA?
WHEN I WAS A LITTLE GIRL I WISHED I HAD THE POWER TO PREVENT BAD PEOPLE FROM HURTING ANYONE.
WITHOUT THE WITCHBLADE, IT'S JUST MY JOB.
BUT WITH IT, I HAVE THE ABILITY TO SAVE OTHERS BEYOND AN INCONCEIVABLE CAPACITY.
THE ONLY DIFFERENCE IS--I'M NOT AFRAID ANYMORE.

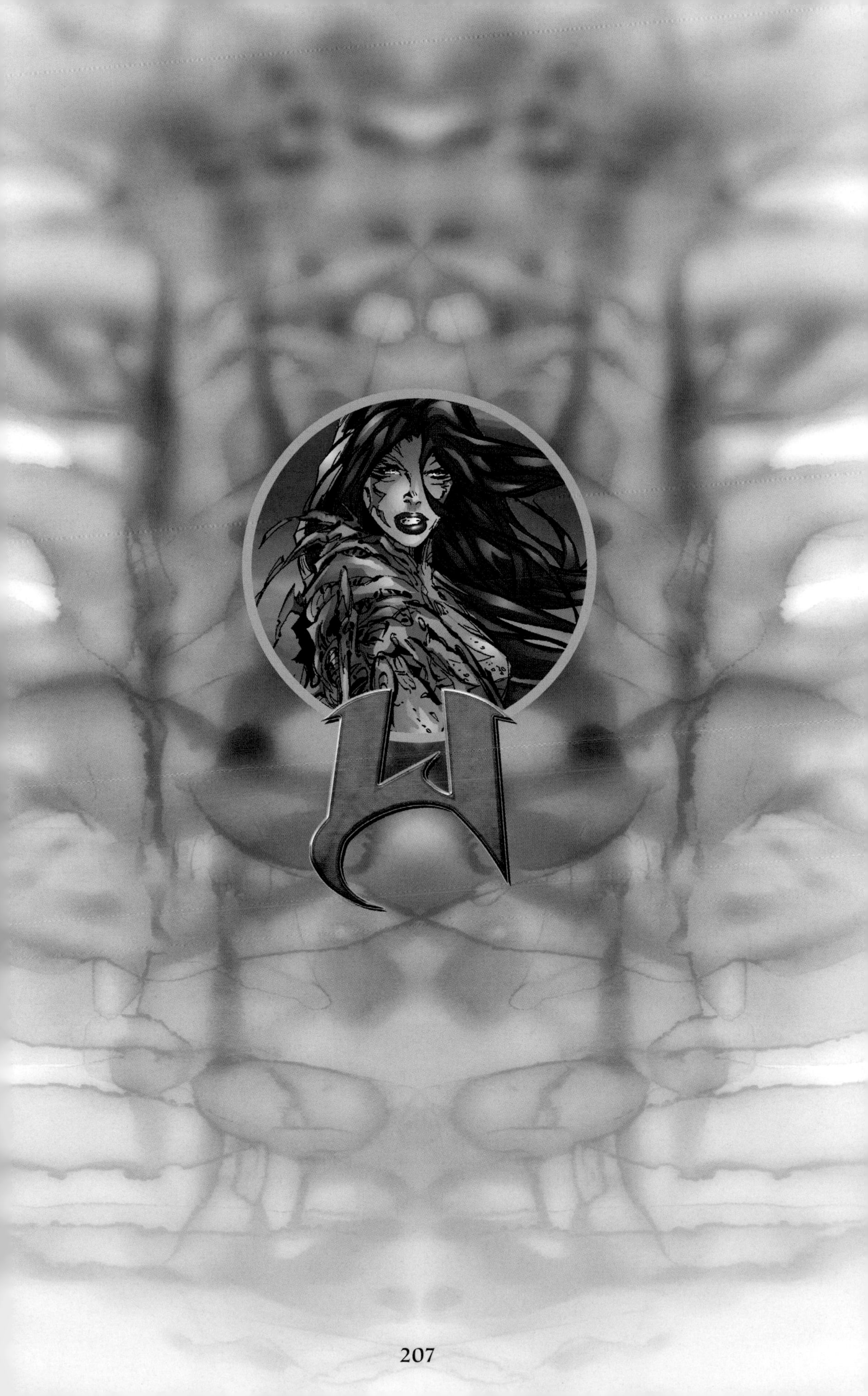

Witchblade: Origins volume 1

# Cover Gallery

*Witchblade* issue #1, wraparound cover
art by: **Michael Turner**
and **Brian Haberlin**

*Witchblade* issue #2
art by: **Michael Turner,**
**D-Tron** and **Juan Carlos**

*Witchblade* issue #3
art by: **Michael Turner, D-Tron**
and **JD Smith**

*Witchblade* issue #4
art by: **Michael Turner, D-Tron**
and **JD Smith**

*Witchblade* issue #5
art by: **Michael Turner, D-Tron**
and **JD Smith**

*Witchblade* issue #6
art by: **Michael Turner**
and **JD Smith**

*Witchblade* issue #7
art by: **Michael Turner, D-Tron**
and **JD Smith**

*Witchblade* issue #8
art by: **Michael Turner, D-Tron**
and **JD Smith**

*Witchblade* issue #1, Wizard Ace™ Edition
art by: **Michael Turner, D-Tron**
and **JD Smith**

*Witchblade* issue #100 variant from
issue #1/2 Overstreet Fan edition variant
art by: **Michael Turner,**
**Marc Silvestri** and **Stjepan Sejic**

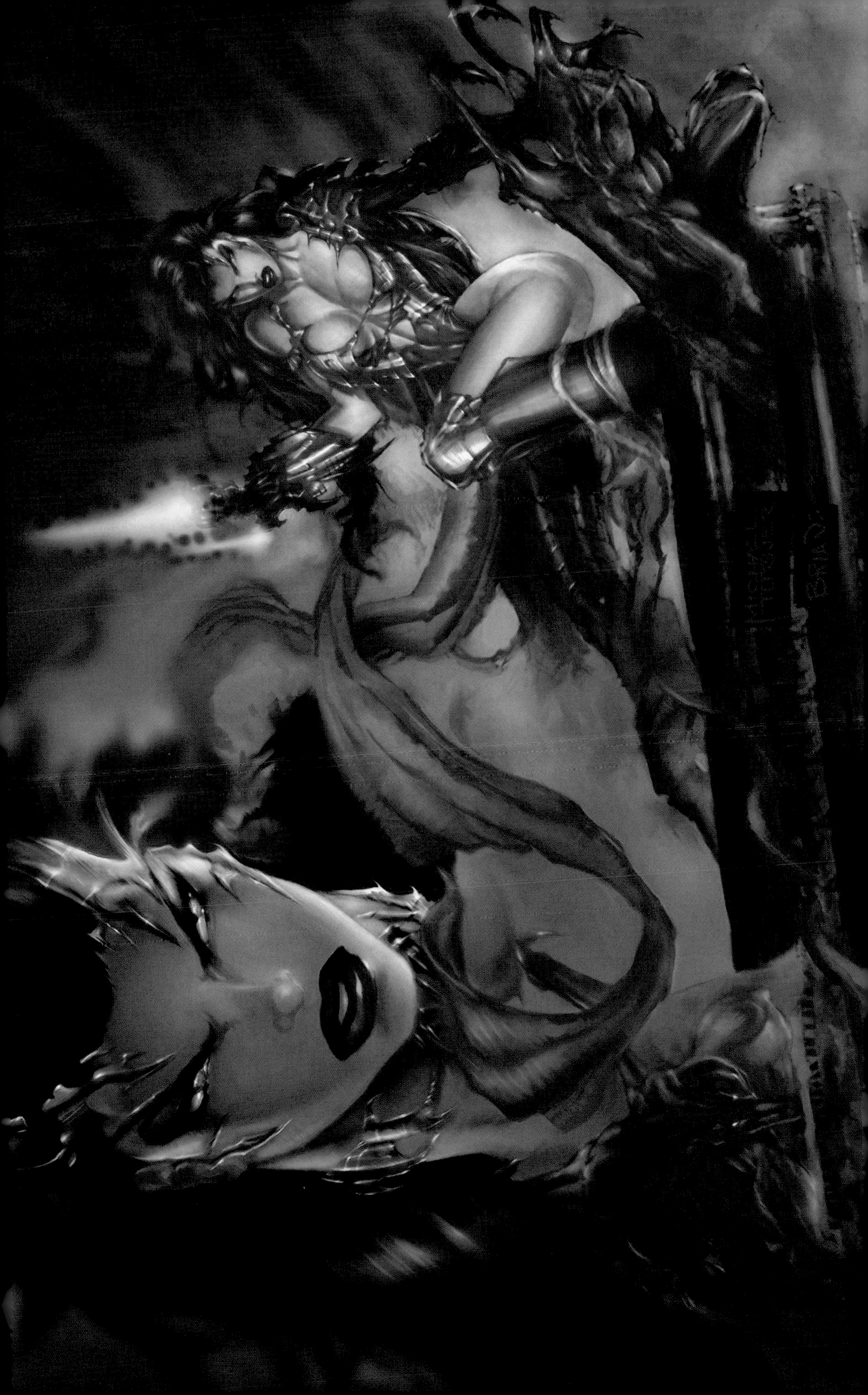

MICHAEL TURNER
'95
D-TRON

MICHAEL TURNER 1995
D-TRON
JD SMITH

MICHAEL TURNER
D-TRON
JD SMITH '95

MICHAEL TURNER
D-TRON.
JD SMITH '96

MICHAEL TURNER 1996
JD SMITH

MICHAEL TURNER
D-TRON
JD SMITH

MICHAEL TURNER
D. TRON
JD SMITH '96

MICHAEL TURNER
D-TRON
SMITH

MICHAEL TURNER
SILVESTRI

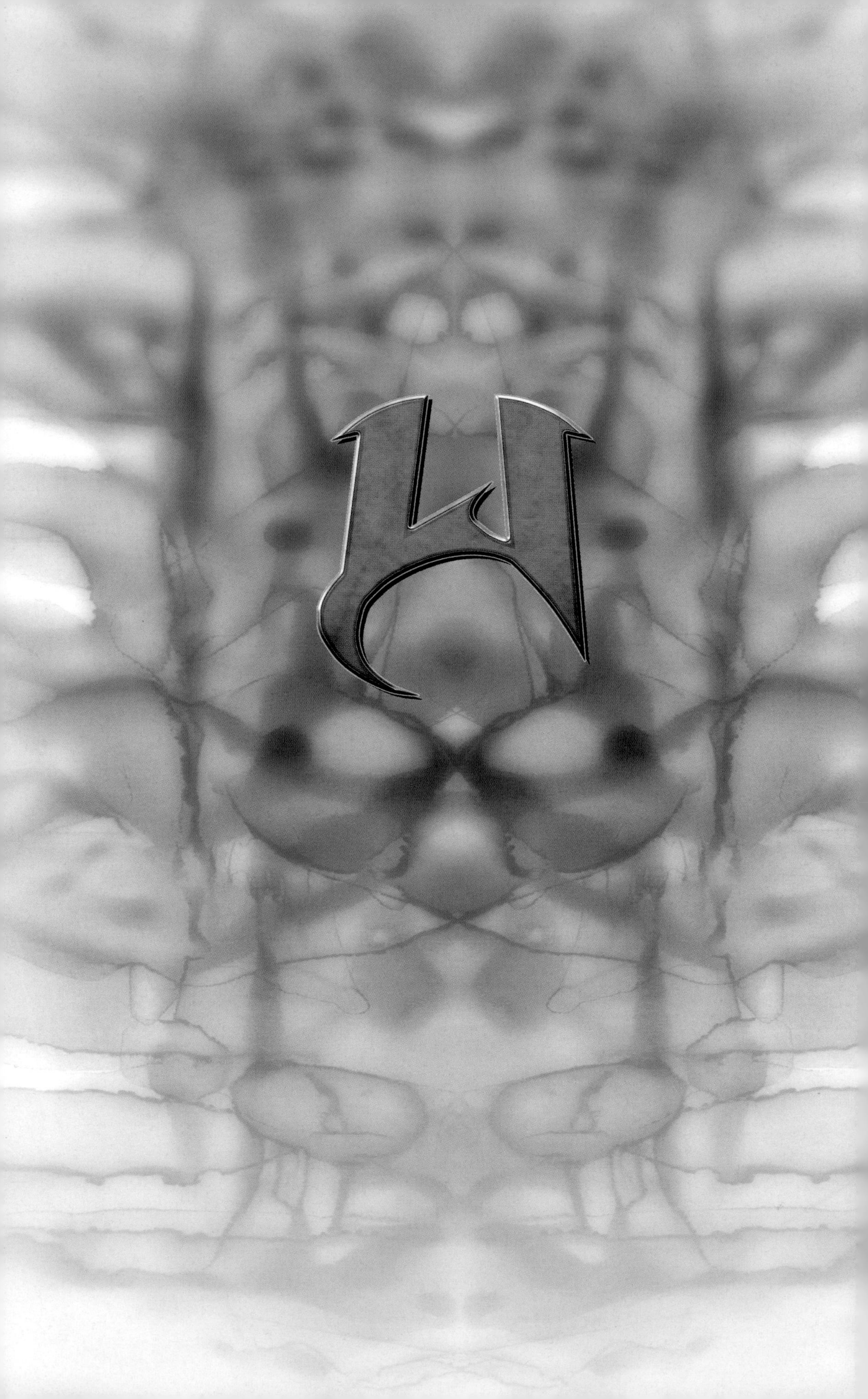

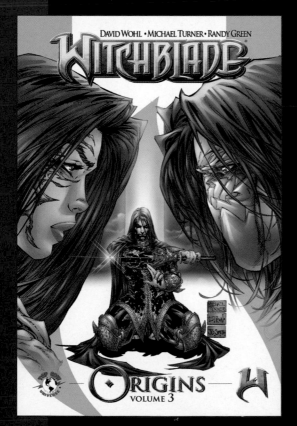

# Premium collected editions

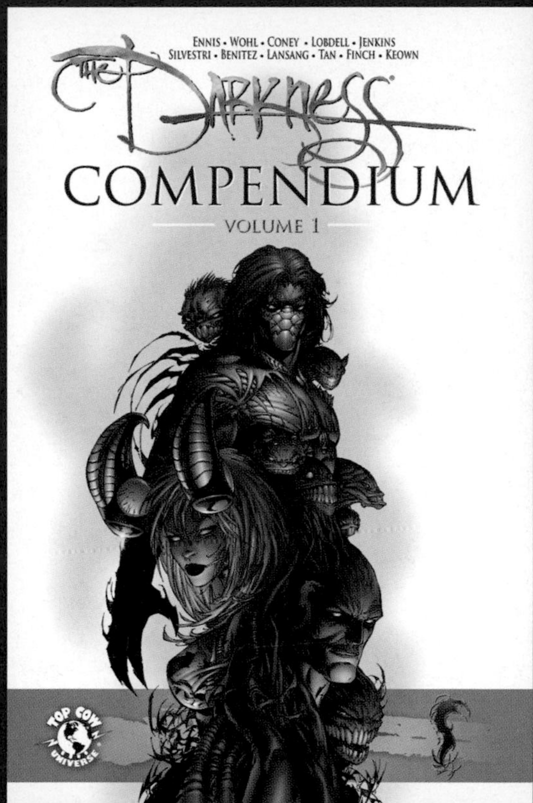


## *The Darkness*

Compendium vol.1

written by:

Garth Ennis, Paul Jenkins, Scott Lobdell

pencils by:

Marc Silvestri, Joe Benitez and more!

On his 21st birthday, the awesome and terrible powers of the Darkness awaken within Jackie Estacado, a mafia hitman for the Franchetti crime family. There's nothing like going back to the beginning and reading it all over again - issues #1-40, plus the complete run of the *Tales of the Darkness* series collected into one trade paperback. See how the Darkness first appeared and threw Jackie into the chaotic world of the supernatural. Get the first appearances of The Magdalena and more!


TP (ISBN 13: 978-1-58240-643-5) $59.99
HC (ISBN 13: 978-1-58240-992-7) $99.99

## *Rising Stars*

Compendium vol.1

written by:

J. Michael Straczynski

pencils by:

Keu Cha, Ken Lashley
Gary Frank, Brent Anderson
and more!

The *Rising Stars* Compendium Edition collects the entire saga of the Pederson Specials, including the entire original series written by series creator J. Michael Straczynski, (*Supreme Power/Midnight Nation*) as well as the three limited series Bright, Voices of the Dead, and Untouchable written by Fiona Avery, (*Amazing Fantasy/No Honor*).

Collects *Rising Stars* issues #0, #1/2, #1-24, Prelude, the short story "Initiations", the limited series *Bright* issues #1-3, *Voices of the Dead* issues #1-6 and *Untouchable* issues #1-5.


TP (ISBN 13: 978-1-58240-802-8) $59.99
HC (ISBN 13: 978-1-58240-[illegible]) $99.99